The Truth Is by Mary Soderstrom

We acknowledge the support of the Canada Council for the Arts, the Ontario Arts Council and the Government of Canada through the Book Publishing Industry Development Program for our publishing activities.

"Frances and Daniel" originally appeared in *Grain*; "Cold Comfort" first appeared in the *Ontario Review* and "Frances Has the Last Word" was originally published, in somewhat different form, in the *Globe and Mail*.

ISBN 0 7780 1159 3 (hardcover)
ISBN 0 7780 1160 7 (softcover)

Cover art by L.L. Fitzgerald
Book design by Michael Macklem

Printed in Canada

PUBLISHED IN CANADA BY OBERON PRESS

In memory of Léa, Leo and Jeanette Roback,
with thanks to Dilshad Engineer and David Helwig

Contents

Park Avenue in Montreal is one of the principal north-south streets in the central part of the city. It runs from downtown, along the eastern edge of Mount Royal, through densely settled neighbourhoods, some of which are gentrifying and some of which are not.

These stories are works of invention. If people and incidents in them remind the reader of true things, the writer has done her job.

1
Truth

Always Assuming That You
Want to Know the Truth

This is an exercise in telling the truth. I have been trying to get it right for many, many years, and now I would like your help. Picture, if you will, the following:

It is the third Thursday in September, a very hot day. Two women in their mid-twenties cross the great hall of Central Station in Montreal. The hall smells of diesel fuel from the locomotives running on the tracks below. There is a small crowd around the stairways at the west end, the ones leading to commuter trains, but it is only mid afternoon, and the end-of-the day rush has not begun.

The dark-haired woman (let us call her Sheila) heads directly for the information desk. She is thin, she has on sunglasses, her tanned legs flash beneath her short, pink cotton dress. The woman who follows her is about as tall, but she does not know where she is going. That lack of certainty, plus her shorter legs, make her look heavy, more earth-bound.

Sheila taps on the counter with her fingernails while she waits for the railway agent to finish with an older woman. They are speaking French and Sheila frowns. Then, as the woman walks away, Sheila doesn't wait for the man to address her. "I want some information about a coffin," she says. She speaks loudly. She has told her friend she does that because it helps to speak loudly with people who speak French.

The man looks at her. So does her friend. Sheila's brother has died; her sunglasses hide presumably tear-stained eyes. She is there to make sure his body makes the connection for the train home to Halifax.

"A coffin," the man repeats. He is greying, heavy-bearded, sad-eyed too. "I don't know anything about coffins."

Sheila looks at him steadily through her sunglasses. "You don't know anything about coffins," she repeats. She does not move, and her friend is not sure what will happen next. Then after a pause the length of a sob, Sheila leans forward, so she can lean on her elbow, supporting her head on her hand. She shakes her head just a little and her shoulders tremble.

Her friend has been dreading this. She has had little experience with grief, she is embarrassed by it, but she knows that this cannot be easy and she would like to help. Things are complicated by the fact that she does not know Sheila very well. She is new to Montreal, there at the station this afternoon because she had not much else to do when Sheila arrived with her story.

"Tomorrow is Friday, he has to get home before sundown on Friday," Sheila tells the man softly, her face hidden. "My mother will be even more upset if he doesn't." Her voice rises slightly. "It's Jewish law," she says. She stops, waiting for a response.

"Look, I can't help you, Miss," the man says, looking straight at her. "I couldn't help you if God the father came down and told me to."

No, I'm sorry. We have to stop here. Sheila's friend is me, Frances, and I suspect I wanted to laugh at that. I can't quite remember, although what I felt is unimportant. What is important is knowing the truth, and I have struggled ever since to remember exactly what happened that afternoon and afterward. It is as if by capturing the details I might find the meaning behind them.

Therefore let us fast forward to a point where things are clearer: the elevator doors open, and Sheila and I walk out into the area where baggage is taken from the trains. It is brightly lit, especially in contrast with the spaces beyond. There the tracks are lost in the darkness of the station.

A man, looking much like the man at the information

9

desk, stands inside a little booth, which must be his office. If he hears the elevator open, he takes no notice. He continues to page through bills of lading or instructions or obscene letters (who can tell after all when things are stuck on a clipboard? All things look official on a clipboard.)

We stand there. The smell of diesel fuel and hot metal is stronger here than it was in the great hall. I also smell myself: the heat has melted my deodorant. My feet in their sandals are filthy. My face is greasy with sweat. I have not been in Montreal long, and I cannot believe this place.

"I'd like some help please," Sheila says very loudly, rapping on the window of the booth.

The man looks up, surprised and annoyed. "What are you doing here?" he asks. Ordinary civilians are not supposed to be here, obviously.

"I came to see about my brother's coffin," Sheila begins. "It's supposed to be put on the train to Halifax tonight, and my mother wants to make sure...."

"Coming from where?" the man says, leafing through his papers.

"Sudbury," Sheila says. She stands up straighter. I think she is bracing herself because it is so hard to repeat what she has to say. "He died day before yesterday and he has to get to Halifax tomorrow because if he comes on Saturday nothing can be done...."

The man listens. Then he looks through his papers again. "I see nothing about a coffin," he says. Flatly, simply: that's that.

Sheila puts her hand up to her eyes. I think she is about to cry, so I begin to talk.

"Call Sudbury," I say to the man. "What time was the coffin sent, Sheila? Do you know what funeral home was handling it?"

She shakes her head. Now both hands are up by her eyes, her purse has slipped down her arm to her elbow. She looks smaller. I feel very sorry for her.

"They're Jewish, and you probably don't know what it means, having a body arrive on Saturday, if you're Jewish," I say, drawing on everything I ever learned from Jewish friends, even from Sheila's roommate Isabelle, who the week before had explained how she, a French-Canadian girl who'd fallen in love with a Jewish man, had converted. "You can't get the body ready for burying, you can't set up the service. And one of the things is, you're supposed to bury people quickly. So her family is caught in the middle. Either way they're in conflict with their beliefs at a time when you need all the support religion can give you...."

I could have gone on. But she puts out her hand to stop me. "No," she says. "That's enough. They'll have it on their conscience. I'll just have to call my mother and...." She doesn't even look at the man. She allows me to put my arm around her She obviously doesn't want me to talk about it anymore.

Tragic scene. She sits slumped against me in the taxi we take back home. We climb the three flights of stairs to our apartments, one next to the other. "Thanks for coming with me," she says, hugs me before she opens her door.

"No problem," I say, turning quickly to open my own. I am embarrassed and sad. I spend the rest of the evening trying to imagine what it would feel like to lose a brother, to be unable to help, to be stranded in Montreal because it costs so much (so Sheila said) to fly back home.

Okay, what would be the lesson if that were the truth, if we stopped right there? Something about bureaucracy and emotion, maybe. What would stick with you would be the heat and the smell and the impossibility of getting anything done. A short description of hell.

But add something else and you change the picture.

Jump forward to Saturday night a week later. (This part I remember better than all the rest, I am clearer about the

11

facts, I hope I am closer to the truth.) My husband and I go to the movies with Sheila and one of her boyfriends. Bernie, he's called. A salesman, our age, presentable looking, whose "th"s come out "d"s: a working-class Montrealer on his way up. He sounds like other people I have known from parts of New York or Philadelphia. People who are Jewish. And so I assume he is.

But then somehow, after the show as we're sitting in Ben's having smoked meat and dill pickles (which reinforces my impression of course), he says his last name: McLaughlin. That is my maiden name, a name which can be Irish or Scotch, Protestant or Catholic. Until then, I have never met a Jewish McLaughlin.

I am amazed, and a little delighted. The smartest people I knew at university were Jewish, and so were the best professors. I would like to think there are Jewish McLaughlins, just as there are Jewish Irishmen like Leopold Bloom.

But when I say so, he is shocked. He isn't Jewish. Jews are…well, different. "Don't get me wrong, I know a lot of them," he says. "But I'm not one. And what's more, Sheila isn't either."

I am flummoxed. I am flabbergasted. I don't know what to say.

"It was a joke," Sheila then tells me, reaching out and patting my hand as if that would change things, would explain the afternoon wandering around the hot station.

"The part about your brother too?" I ask meekly. Yes, I must admit: I felt meek, unstable, out of my depth.

She nods and smiles at Bernie. Her message is that I am the flake, not her.

Or maybe she only looks at me with surprise: "You were mistaken."

Whatever, I am struck dumb. I sit there, watching my husband squirm, feeling stupid, too shocked to make a scene. We finish our drinks, our sandwiches and we leave,

12

smiling, as if nothing had happened. It is only later that I begin to wonder why she lied and what exactly is the truth.

I did not want to see Sheila after that, and because I was not working I could arrange things to avoid her. In the mornings I waited until her door slammed and I could hear her heels hurrying down the stairs before I went out. When I heard her voice in the front entrance, I went around behind the building to come in through the garage.

Her roommate was a different matter. She was small and blond and smiled all the time. What is more, she let me try to speak to French to her. We didn't talk about anything deep: the weather, how quickly it got cold at the end of October, the terrible way the janitor kept the stairway. But I looked forward to my conversations with her as much as I did anything else that winter. I'd be lying if I didn't say there was some economic motive too: I found a job by mid-November but it was rotten. I needed French if I was going to get anything more interesting and better paying: English secretarial work was the pits.

We didn't talk much about Sheila. I certainly didn't mention the coffin and Bernie McLaughlin, because I didn't want to seem so stupid, and because the fact that Isabelle was Jewish, a recent Jew even, made me wonder if she'd be offended by the story. Which was a lie after all.

And it certainly seemed that she and Sheila weren't getting on very well. Isabelle wasn't there much—she must be spending weekends with her boyfriend I decided. But I heard things. The way the apartments were laid out, a conversation in their entry hall could be heard in our living-room, an angry word spoken in Isabelle's bedroom was clearly audible in our spare room.

You are probably right to ask about the truth again at this point. What I am going to tell you now is no more than eavesdropping and rumours. Hearsay, inadmissible in court. The very fact that I admit to listening casts a shadow

13

on me, doesn't it? Nevertheless I did.

I heard the janitor come up the first time and ask about the rent for January, and Sheila say, smooth as you like, that Isabelle was supposed to take care of that. Isabelle wasn't there.

Isabelle wasn't there the second time either, but she was the third, a week later, early in the morning before any of us had gone to work. I was in the kitchen putting coffee in a Thermos (I could save more than a dollar a day bringing my own coffee and we needed every extra dime.) My husband thought that it was me yelling, that I'd scalded myself or cut myself when Isabelle started screaming. But it wasn't.

She had a big voice for a little person, and she was furious. The money, she said, had been given to Sheila. Sheila had been supposed to pay the rent. Sheila was lying if she'd told the man that Isabelle had taken care of it. Sheila lied a lot, and Isabelle had had enough of it.

The man backed down, blasted by her words perhaps. But not before he called up the stairs; "Your name's on the lease, though, you know; you're responsible. Your girlfriend pointed that out to me."

Or so I think now.

"That Sheila," my husband said. "What rock did she crawl out from under?" Then he left, because he had to get to work. So did I, and I ran the rest of the way down the stairs when I heard Sheila's door open as I was leaving. Don't want to see her, I said over and over to myself. Don't want to see her.

I counted myself lucky because I didn't see either one of them for a couple of days. Then, when I took our own rent by on the first of February, I met Isabelle coming out of the janitor's apartment. She looked at me once, hard, but then she smiled. "Bonjour," she said.

I bonjoured right back, and tried to think of how you

said the weather was improving. But she was gone, and, to be truthful, I was glad.

Our lease ran to the end of June, and my husband started agitating for a move to some place where we wouldn't have traffic all night just outside our windows. Finding a new place fell to me, of course: he was trying to finish up his master's thesis, he didn't have the time to work at his job and on it, let alone look for apartments. He explained that all very carefully, but I was mad anyway so I didn't look very hard. In fact I rebelled one Saturday morning when he went off to his office to work on his thesis, leaving me with the classified ads open to the apartments-to-let section. I stayed in bed and slept. Then, near noon I got up and took a long bath. It was early afternoon before I sat down at the desk in the spare room to write some letters.

The building was quiet, and the windows were closed tight because it was Siberian outside. The only noise in the room was the scratch of my pen on the paper: the last thing I wanted to do was type on my day off. Then I heard the groans. Not loud and not frightening. Maybe not groans at all. But sounds, animal-like. Lovers? I asked myself. Isabelle and her boyfriend? I was prepared to be embarrassed. And then Isabelle cried again: "Out, out."

I sat very quietly. The floor creaked, a door closed. Water ran somewhere. Then Sheila yelled something as she banged in their coat closet. The front door opened, slammed. Footsteps on the stairs: light and quick. Sheila, certainly.

I held my breath, waiting. There seemed to be silence on the other side of the wall. Then the phone rang. Reluctantly I got up to answer it in the kitchen; there was an extension in the spare room but now that I had heard what I had, I didn't want anyone on the other side to hear me.

It was my husband, not at all upset that I was still there, glad in fact. He'd got a coffee to go with his sandwich (he didn't like to carry a Thermos and I'd not been awake to see

15

that he had his that morning, remember) and started talking to a guy from another division in the lunch-room. His mother had a duplex to rent beginning in early June. Maybe we ought to go look at it that afternoon?

Sure, of course, why not? Anything to get away from the memory of the groans on the other side of the wall, whatever they might have been. I wanted to forget them, I didn't want to tell him about them. I wanted out of this place. That last is probably the truest statement in all I have told you so far. I wanted out. I had had enough. I would have agreed to look at any place, I would have met him anywhere.

But before I left I stopped for a moment to listen in the spare room. Silence still on the other side. I did not know if that was good or bad.

It doesn't really matter what the apartment looked like, it wouldn't do, it was too far away from the Metro and one winter here had taught us to stay close to enclosed public transportation if you want to get around in all weathers. My husband was disappointed. So was I, I guess.

But not nearly as much as I was when we met Sheila on the stairs.

"Oh, hello," she said, beaming and fussing with her handbag. "Listen, you don't have $20 I could borrow until tomorrow? I gave my last cash to Isabelle last night and I haven't got enough to take a taxi to my boyfriend's."

I pushed by her without speaking. I wasn't going to give money to her, the liar. Who knows where she was going or what she'd done to be broke? But my husband stopped to listen.

"He's expecting me for dinner," she said. "And then we're going to the Centaur Theatre to see the show, you know which one I mean, the one that got the good reviews. But I'm running late, and I really have to get there on time to play hostess, you know, he's asked his boss over and he wants to make a good impression and...."

He pulled out his wallet and handed her two $5 bills, without saying anything. She grabbed them and was down the stairs. "Thanks ever so much, you really are a life-saver, I'll pay you back the first of the week...."

I saved my comments until we were in the apartment: I didn't want any of the other neighbours to hear. But before I could tell him how stupid giving money to her was, I heard the alarm clock ringing. At first I thought it was in our spare room, but once I went in there, I could tell the sound was coming through the wall.

My husband followed me in the room. I turned around and looked at him as he listened. Then he looked at his wristwatch. "Five o'clock on Saturday afternoon," he said, shaking his head.

"Strange," I said. And then because—I don't know why —I turned and went back out of our apartment and into the hall. You could hear the alarm out there too.

He followed me, and for a second we looked at each other, unsure what to do next. Then I reached for the door handle. It turned easily and the door swung open.

What did I find? I don't remember, to tell you the truth. The light on in the kitchen, I think. Isabelle's room, a mess, with the sheets and blankets pulled on the floor, the window shade still down. I hit the alarm to turn it off as I quickly looked around the room. No Isabelle, though.

My husband found her in the bathtub. There was a note in lipstick on the mirror for her boyfriend: I'm filthy, it said. I'm not good enough for you. I am unclean.

I remember looking from that to her, lying in the tub, all blue around the mouth, but with a slight yellow tint to the rest of her skin. Only the tips of her breasts showing pink where they floated above the surface of the pink water. Dead, I thought. She's dead. I grabbed for my husband, I know that, and we stood clinging to each other for a mo-

17

ment trying to decide what to do.

But we must not have remained paralyzed long because the ambulance crew was able to save her when they arrived. She was still breathing, thank goodness, with only superficial wounds on her wrists; it's hard to succeed in slashing wrists, I know now. The cold water slowed the bleeding down, too, and the drugs that she took worked against each other. But if we hadn't come in, she would have gone on dying and she might have succeeded.

A happy ending perhaps? A couple of months later she met somebody else, and the next winter she got married. A Jewish wedding with her psychiatrist as a guest. That much I know, that much I know is true.

And Sheila? What is the truth about her?

That is where my tunnelling after what really happened comes up against sheer, impenetrable rock. This is where I need help the most.

I hear her clicking down the stairs in her high heels, I see her walking away from me quickly, her legs flashing beneath her short skirt. Sunglasses on even though it is now winter. Nervous. Excitable. Guilty.

Maybe she called from Ottawa on Monday night. Maybe she said she was worried, that she'd called and called all Sunday, but Isabelle didn't answer. "What's going on?" she might have asked, as if she didn't know.

I might have told her. "But what are you doing there? The last time I saw you, you were going out to dinner? Haven't you been back?"

There would be a silence, in which I might imagine the wheels turning. "No," she would say finally. "No. Like I said I was on my way to my boyfriend's, I mean I hadn't even stuck my head in the door so I didn't see...." She might pause, and I would almost hear her try and figure out what to say. "You see, what happened, well, what happened...."

"I don't believe you," I would say no matter what she

18

said. "I don't believe a word you say."

There might be silence on the other end of the line. "Oh," she would say. Her voice would be high and light, a child's voice. "Well, in that case then, you can go tell that Jewish bitch to fuck herself. Tell her she should be glad that her boyfriend doesn't know the truth."

Truth, truth: what truth?

I don't remember if it happened like that. I only know I hung up first. I only know I never saw her again.

These days I live in a neighbourhood where to be Jewish is not a thing to be taken lightly. Most of us aren't, but those who are are among the most pious in the world. Every family has a grandfather with a number tattooed on the inside of his arm. Some have grandmothers who survived the camps, too. But they are much younger than their husbands, they are second wives, taken after the War was over because the first wives died along with the youngest children: they couldn't keep up, they were no use in the factories. So there are no women in their eighties or late seventies, nor are there any adults my age—or the age that Sheila would be now. What few babies were born in those War years just didn't live.

If Sheila had known that would she have pretended to be Jewish? Or was that what she wanted all along?

Thank you. Your attention has been a comfort, even though the truth seems no clearer to me now than when I began. There is no end in sight, no ending either, no matter how I hold bits of the story up to the light to see what sort of pattern they make. I would like to find a moral, because life is always easier if the stories you tell have a moral. But morals are as hard to decipher as the truth is to find.

And the nearest I can come to the truth now is what I heard the talking heads last night say on the news. (The news is the truth, isn't it? The talking heads help us judge what happens, don't they?) It is winter again, and there is a woman who is camped out beneath a pine tree in an open space by the Place des Arts Metro, where the 80 bus stops. She refuses to go to a shelter, even though it is so cold that she hasn't come out from beneath her plastic bags and boxes for the last week. A de-institutionalized psychiatric patient, one of the heads said. First name: Sheila. Last name: unknown.

I wonder...I wonder. But then I stop myself. People have gone mad wondering. People have gone mad looking for the truth.

The truth, the truth. Tell me, do you think it ever matters?

Testimony from Men Who Knew Her

BARRY: Elaine had an expensive wool coat. I knew what it cost; when you're in the fur trade you keep an eye on what the competition is charging. She had nice leather boots too, which obviously she took good care of.

She had on just a jacket, though, when I picked her up even though it was snowing. I know now it's because she'd forgotten and left her winter things downstairs when she came in after work so she couldn't get them when she snuck out. But then I was just pleased because it gave me a reason to swing by the office, and get the fur coat.

She wasn't thrilled about going back and she wanted to wait in the car but I told her it wasn't safe after dark in the parking-garage and she came along with me. She sat on the desk, one leg crossed over the other, and when I turned back to her, I've got to tell you I wouldn't have minded not going any further that night. Great legs.

However, I knew better than to try anything just then.

"Here," I said, holding out the coat. She'd seen it, she'd even tried it on when Mme Simard brought it in to exchange for a new model. "You're going to freeze tonight. Try this on."

Well, right away I saw her eyes light up. The coat had looked terrific on her and she was a girl who knew quality.

"Take it," I said. "It's yours."

She hesitated just a minute before she stood up. She didn't say anything, just turned around and stood with her back to me. She took off her jacket slowly, almost like she was afraid to. But then she held out her arms so I could slip the coat on her. And then she stood, holding the collar up to her face and rubbing her cheek against the fur.

She was beautiful and I was very pleased at what I'd done.

So we went to Altitude 727, up on top of Place Ville Marie, for a drink and looked out the windows at the snow swirling around, making the city white. Beautiful. I told her she was a princess in a magic tower, with all the world to command. I told her I would do anything for her. I told her....

And she didn't say very much. She listened, and she didn't giggle which I've seen a lot of girls do in similar circumstances. Definitely a class act. She just sat there with the coat on the chair beside her, and her black hair slicked behind her ears so that you could see her throat, all white and vulnerable.

So you can see it was all going very well. But then I had to make my move. Across the street to the Queen Elizabeth Hotel, in the snow, to have a room-service supper.

We came out on the plaza and the snow was three inches deep, sticking to everything, making it look like something out of, I don't know, a magazine or something. But of course she didn't have any boots on so I picked her up and carried her across the square and then across the street. Good thing I work out regularly. She was impressed, I think, and I wasn't even breathing all that hard—at least not as hard as I expected to later.

Which I did. She was ready to go to one of the restaurants for supper, but I picked up the key for the room I'd reserved earlier, and I sort of just pulled her by the hand toward the elevators and she came with me without protesting. A class act, let me tell you. She knew how to do it.

MR. BARRETT: Catherine found the coat Monday. She wasn't cleaning in Elaine's room, she'd given up on that some time before. No, she was looking for something she thought Elaine might have borrowed: a red mohair scarf I believe that Catherine was particularly fond of and Elaine was always forgetting to return.

I don't know how much Catherine'd gone through looking for the scarf. All I know was that I was eating breakfast in the kitchen late and alone. Then through the sound of the CBC news on the radio, I heard Catherine scream.

I ran upstairs, sure that she'd hurt herself badly, but there she stood in one piece but screaming, with the coat in her arms like a dead animal.

My first thought was that Elaine had stolen it. The other possibility didn't occur to me, and when Catherine jumped to the correct conclusion I found it almost comforting. Theft is worse than promiscuity. The prison sentences are longer.

But Catherine quite correctly had to find out who had given it to Elaine and what she had done in return. Oh, there are families where the sexual behaviour of children is of little concern to the parents once the younger generation has reached a certain age. But ours is not one of them. What is more, neither Catherine nor I were aware Elaine was seeing someone seriously enough for a gift of this magnitude to be considered. And if she did not want us to know about him, there was sure to be a reason, a reason which would trouble us greatly.

"It was under the bed, wrapped in a sheet," Catherine said when she calmed down enough to speak. "Under the bed, like in a third-rate mystery."

We didn't immediately connect the coat with her job, but frankly we didn't have much idea of where she was working. She was a receptionist for a garment manufacturer on St. Lawrence Blvd, that we knew. But what kind of garments I never asked, and she never said. She found the job herself, she was inordinately proud of that fact, and when we tried to point out that she'd be better paid as a receptionist in an insurance company or a typist at McGill, she wouldn't listen to us. So we let her be pig-headed. After all, a garment manufacturer is a garment manufacturer and the job was boring. She'd change her mind about what she

23

ought to do with her life soon enough, I was sure.

Of course, as the winter developed we had hints that things were not as they should be. Her brother had seen her in Rockhead's, a jazz club in a completely unsuitable neighbourhood. With a man who was much older.

The question of course arises why it would be all right for her brother to be there (and I didn't ask him who he was with, I didn't even think to ask until Elaine wanted to know what he was doing there). To be perfectly just I suppose I ought to be concerned about him too. But he is four years older than she, he is doing quite respectably at university, he is reliable. She, of course, would not listen to that. She said she was eighteen after all, and old enough to go out with whomever she wished. She was going to move out, she couldn't take being treated like a child.

That was when my blood ran cold. How could she move out? Where would she live? She certainly wasn't making enough to pay rent herself, and what sort of person would she end up sharing an apartment with? Maybe if we'd sat down with her then, if Catherine had helped her work out a budget, she would have seen just how impossible it was. But we didn't. We reacted. I reacted.

She was grounded. She was forbidden to go out after supper for a month, she was to go to work and then come home. Her salary she could keep, she wouldn't have to pay the small contribution we'd been asking from her (with the vain idea that that would help her become more responsible). No, she could keep the money. But until she demonstrated that we could trust her, she couldn't spend it.

We didn't talk it over with the other children, any more than we said anything about our disappointment that she'd done so poorly in school and had been so stubborn about finding a job that really offered no future. Was that a mistake? Could they have warned us?

THE TAXI DRIVER: Sure, I picked her up oh, maybe half

24

a dozen times that winter. You might not think that would be much, but I saw her more often than that. She'd come out of the building where she worked and wait on the corner for the bus. She stood out. Like Snow White, you know: that black hair and the white skin with the red, red lips. I didn't notice the blue eyes until the first time she got in my cab, but I saw how she used to wear that same colour of blue. Her winter coat was that blue, sort of bright, almost cheerful, like a summer sky only darker.

Nice description, eh? My wife says I've got the soul of a poet. I sing some, too. My own songs. That's what I really want to do, you know. Driving cab is only a way to make some money. Gives you flexibility though. You can do other things if you've got a mind to.

But anyway, I didn't know her name but sometimes I'd see her waiting for the bus while I waited at the stand just around the corner. At 4:30, 5:00, it was a pretty good place to pick up fares. Not the women who do the work in the factories, of course. Most of them are straight off the boat, haven't got two cents to rub together. They take the bus or walk home, no matter what the weather. But the salesmen and the girls who work in the offices are a different story. They've got more money, first of all. And they're supposed to look nice, even the girls. Waiting out in the rain or the snow is definitely not the sort of thing they want to do.

The first time I picked her up, I had my guitar in the front seat. I don't usually travel with it. Takes up too much space. But the next day some friends and I were going to sing, you know, at a talent night. Nothing big, you know, just a bar that on Tuesdays lets people perform. They pass the hat afterwards. Never make any money, but it's all right to try every once in a while. So I had the guitar and when things were really slow I practiced a little.

So, anyway, she got in and gave an address in West-mount, which surprised me a little because while she was

25

nice looking she looked a little too flashy to be somebody's daughter from Westmount and I was sure she wasn't making enough money working where she was to pay her own way there. But you don't argue with customers, you just go where they want.

It was pretty wet, it was one of those steady, grey rains that you think will never stop, but you don't want to stop really, because you know the next step on the stations of the year will be winter.

"Stations of the year:" that's from one of my songs. Not bad, eh?

And she asked about the guitar, and I told her about playing, and she asked where the club was like she was real interested. So I told her and I sang a couple of verses for her, and then we were in Westmount, on one of those short little streets that parallel Sherbrooke. Decent enough neighbourhood, but not the best.

That was the first time. The others I never had the guitar with me, but she always asked how it was going....

Oh, maybe I gave her a ride two, three times after the first of the year. Sure I noticed that she wasn't wearing the blue coat anymore. You noticed what she was wearing, she was that kind of person. I figured that she must have been promoted or something. That's what they do, you know. They hire a girl for office work and then they have her model things when they need to show them off to a client. Then maybe if things are going good and the girl has something special they switch her over to doing shows, to modelling, maybe even doing some of the design work. And all the time she's still expected to answer the phone and maybe type the letters. They don't usually give her any more money for the extra work, but there are enough girls who like the glamour that they can get away with it.

So I thought the coat was one of the perks. It was, I guess but not for the work she was doing at the office.

26

THE DOCTOR: I wasn't surprised to see her when she came into the office, but apparently she was to see me. We'd met at a reception her uncle had given. He is one of my colleagues at the hospital and I'd gone, largely because my wife Emily was still in the Islands and I was bored. I thought Elaine was one of the maids, she was wearing a black dress with a white collar and passing around a plate of hors d'oeuvres. And being temporarily alone, I'd had a nice little chat with her.

But she hadn't come in as a follow-up to our meeting at her uncle's, it turned out. One of the girls she worked with gave her my office number. It seems I have a very good reputation among working girls: heaven will protect them after all.

She had a vivid memory of our little conversation however, I could tell, and after our professional chat was over she agreed to meet me in the lobby of my building in about an hour to have a drink together. Emily was still away, and I was a bit at loose ends. So was she, I had the feeling. And my instincts are rarely wrong. All those years of dealing with women and their problems have given me a great understanding. That sounds presumptuous but it's true.

At any rate, I made out her prescription after a rather quick examination. Yes, of course, the nurse was present, or if she wasn't she was just in the room outside. I run a very professional practice, you know. I don't mix business and pleasure, you may be sure. But I did do the examination, as I think you will find is recommended in all the literature on birth control pills. She was a healthy young woman, no longer a virgin, but not pregnant, and probably not terribly experienced. You can tell that from the way a woman comports herself, and from the state of her tissues.

And that was all that day. We had a chat, a drink, and then she said she had to go, that her parents expected her home by a certain hour, I forget what exactly. That surprised me a bit, because it's rare for a woman of her age, and of her, um, comportment to be tied to her parents. But she said it with a certain ironic grin and I was half persuaded that she was joking. She might have been going to meet someone else, I remember thinking. The young burn the candle at both ends, you know. She might be ready to be quite charming to me but hold out just as much charm to someone else. You have to expect that. So I kissed her, like an uncle, on the cheek and saw her into a cab.

BARRY: She didn't tell me about the drama that her parents made over the coat. She should have, I know about parents, I know about fights. My family is one continual fight which is why I see them only on Friday nights for an hour and a half even though I work for my father. The family scene is just too much.

But she didn't say anything to me. She showed up at work one day with a twisted ankle, though. Said she'd slipped on the ice. It wasn't until just at the end that she told me how she'd been sneaking out, and how she slipped on the fire escape. God, can you imagine? She'd climb out her window onto the balcony, then give herself a boost up to the roof. After that she had the roofs of five houses to cross, walking carefully near the edges so that she would make as little noise as possible inside. Then she'd step across the three-foot gap between the roof of the last house and the fire escape on the apartment building on the corner. She'd been doing it since she was a kid, she said she and her brother and sister used to play hide and seek up there. But once, toward the end of February when she was coming back from a club with me, she slid the last three stairs and turned her ankle. God, it gives me the willies just to think about it. She could have broken her neck.

Yeah, I know it comes to the same thing, in a way. But if you're going to die young, you ought to have packed a whole lot of life into your time. And she did. And I helped her, I suppose.

Like I said, she was a class act, and you could take her anywhere. Some of the bimbos can really embarrass you. Talk dirty and loud, you know, things like that. But Elaine could walk across a room, so cool and beautiful, and everybody would look at her. She would listen to what you had to say too. But you had to be careful to stay on her good side, because if you didn't, she'd just walk out on you. She told me once, when she'd got up and left a club right in the middle of a set, that she didn't see any reason why she should waste her time being bored.

And the sex. Yes, I know it's probably central to the whole business, but it's kind of hard to talk about. Hey, how do you like that, me not wanting to talk about sex! I've had my share, I know what I'm talking about when I talk about it. Elaine was special though. She had—no, wait a minute, it sounds stupid, but there's only one way to put it. She had a gift for sex. She said once she wanted to be a dancer because then she would be like making love in public, for the whole world. She said that after we'd spent an afternoon in the apartment of a friend of mine, and we'd tried everything, every place. It was like dancing, with her, all grace and strength and beauty.

My mother knew she was special. Not that my mother knew who she was, I don't even think my dad said anything about me seeing a girl from the business. He didn't like that. He didn't mind when I messed around a little (I suppose he did a bit himself, at least when he was younger), but he thought it was bad business to get serious. Unless of course I wanted to get married. And maybe I did, which is maybe what my mother sensed. "Bring her home," she said to me one Friday when I wouldn't wait to have coffee and dessert with them after dinner. "Unless you're ashamed of her. Bring her home even if you're ashamed of her. I'd like

29

to know the worse before it goes any further."

But anyway, I didn't know that she was pregnant, I really didn't. She was taking the pill, she told me after the first time, so I didn't worry too much about condoms and things (the disease business wasn't an issue: she was such a lady, she was obviously so clean). And if I'd known she was pregnant, I would have done the right thing, you know. I would have brought her home, I would have married her, I would have made an honest woman of her, and told my mother to keep her remarks to herself.

MR. BARRETT: There was no reasoning with her. She refused to give the coat back, she refused to stop seeing whomever it was, she refused to tell us anything at all.

Poor Catherine was beside herself. I don't know when I've seen her so upset. But what after all were our options? Let Elaine continue, let her move out, try to punish her? Well, I agree that we couldn't let her move out. That would have been worse, God knows who she would have fallen in with. And she was eighteen, I don't quite know how we could have controlled her more closely. So after the tears and the storms, we agreed to let her keep the coat. But the curfew remained. And, like fools, I suppose we thought we had convinced her that it was for her own good, and when she promised she'd stay in her room except for Friday and Saturday nights we believed her. Friday and Saturday she walked out the door with the coat on, brazen as could be, and Catherine worried all evening until Elaine's key turned in the lock. Neither of us realized that she went out after that, or that she went out the other nights too.

But I ask you again, what could we have done?

THE DOCTOR: We met twice after she came to my office. The first time I ran into her at noon in Ogilvy's where she was at the cosmetics counter which was right on the way to the men's wear, if you remember. I was picking up some new shirts: with Emily away I seemed never to get to the laundry and I was always running out.

She shook hands. Not many girls do that. Oh, a French-speaking girl will give you two kisses perhaps, but I can't think of any other woman under 25 who shakes hands unless she's trying to make a business deal. Pity. It's a charming custom. At any rate as she stood there, I held her hand just a trifle longer than necessary because I was so pleasantly impressed. Then I said something about how she had no need to spend her time or money preparing herself because she was lovely enough as it was. And she laughed that lovely laugh.

She'd had lunch already, as it turned out, but I persuaded her to come with me to Toman's, the Czech café just around the corner for coffee and pastry. A charming place too, and just right for taking the first step, I find. The next time I saw her was when I took her to a dinner the following week. The hostess was an old friend, an old mistress actually, someone whom Emily dislikes intensely. I was sure we would find no-one who knew Elaine, and no-one who would care with whom I arrived. But I thought Elaine would be amusing in such company. She was.

And that is all. I assure you my interest in her was far from predatory. Certainly I made no advances that she did not indicate would be well received. I am, I insist, a gentleman and what is more, a man who loves women in the most admirable sense of the word.

But, I am sad to say, she must have come across others who were not so gentle with her. The afternoon of the accident she did indeed call at my office. She was pregnant, she wanted an abortion. I am afraid I could not help her just then. Wait, I said, there are solutions, but you must follow the proper procedures. She would have nothing of that, however. My nurse said she left in tears.

THE TAXI DRIVER: I hadn't seen her in that part of town before, and when she hailed me, I cut off the guy behind

31

me so I could pick her up. Hadn't seen her at all for a while, except once getting into the BMW of some little guy. Hmm, I remember thinking, so somebody's got his hooks into her.

She was crying. She had the fur coat on, even though the day had turned warm. A foretaste of spring, *un avant-goût*, like they say in French. You'd like to think that there will be daffodils and tulips not far in the future, but you know that you've got a couple of months of slush and mud before winter really is over. Still, you can't help hoping.

Obviously, though, the weather had no positive effect on her spirits. She didn't even notice who I was when she climbed in, although, like I said, always before she recognized me. I had to ask her "where to," too. It was like she was completely beside herself.

The voice must have twigged something, though, because she looked up and caught my eyes in the rear-view mirror. "Oh," she said, "it's you."

"You want to go home?" I asked.

"You remember where?" she asked back.

I smiled at her because she looked so forlorn and a smile was all I could offer her. "Sure," I said. "You're not the kind you forget."

She kind of stared at me for a moment longer, as if she really couldn't take things in very well. Then she started fumbling in her purse. "Listen," she said. "How much would you charge just to drive around for a while. Up to Westmount Summit maybe, or down along the river."

"How much you got?" I asked, figuring. It was the middle of the afternoon. Things usually were pretty dead.

She opened her wallet and held out a couple of bills. "Not much," she said. "Ten dollars and some change...?"

Things are pretty dead, I repeated to myself. I had been ready to take a break. I put down the flag. "I'll let it run for $5 worth, and if you want to keep going after that, we'll worry about that later," I said.

She nodded, didn't even smile, but she seemed to relax a little.

Spring-like day, the best place to go is the top of the mountain, so I turned around and headed up that way. She didn't say much for a while, just sat there and sniffled a little. But I knew it would be good for her to talk about it, whatever it was. "Always remember," I said finally, "out of the mud grows the lotus."

That caught her attention. "What?" she said, wiping her eyes and her nose.

"Out of the mud grows the lotus. Words to live by. Means that good things can come out of bad ones. Something to remember when you've got problems."

She leaned back against the seat and looked out the windows. "Ah," she said. "The wisdom of the east."

"Don't know. I saw it first written on a wall in Old Montreal."

She gave just a suspicion of a smile. "Can I tell you about it?"

"Sure," I said. "I thought that's why you wanted to go for a ride."

So we drove around for the better part of an hour and she told me all about it. Barry, and her parents, and the doctor. Particularly the doctor. I think she would have been all right if it hadn't been for him.

THE DOCTOR: But I assure you my conduct in my offices has never been anything but completely professional. I have never made any secret about my private life. In the circles I frequent, one's amorous adventures are forgiven provided one is discreet. I have always been discreet.

And the patient-doctor relationship is something sacred, you know. The allegations of the taxi driver are groundless.

MR. BARRETT: Yes, I suppose we failed her. Whether we

should have been less severe or more severe, we will never know.

Catherine was devastated, of course. In spite of the fact that she was quite a different person—in character more like our oldest daughter, calm and intellectual—I think she identified quite a bit with Elaine. There was the physical resemblance of course, which was striking. More than once when I was concentrating on a problem, I would look up or come into a room and see Elaine and somehow feel myself lost in time because she looked so much like Catherine. Maybe that's why I worried so about her.

At least Catherine is still there, at least she didn't run away.

THE TAXI DRIVER: Actually I thought I had cheered her up. At the top of Westmount Summit we got out and walked over to look at the city. The sun was already low by then, it was late afternoon, we'd been driving around a lot longer than I'd expected. But the light was sort of transparent and the sky was that blue that promises, oh, I don't know, joy, I guess. Like her eyes, only lighter.

"So," she said, "I'm finished with men." She wrapped the coat around her a little tighter because in the shadows it was getting cold already. Then she leaned forward and looked out at the city, the skeletons of trees, the river, the bridges, and beyond, the hills sticking out of the plain like fists.

My wife has said that when she's fed up with me or with her father or with our boys. We both know she doesn't mean it, we're good friends, and the sex part is good, too. But I really didn't know this girl. So I said: "Hey, you don't mean that!" With an exclamation point. Be sure and put the exclamation point in.

She looked over at me and I could see how your average guy's response would be full speed ahead. She didn't need that from me, for sure. So I said: "Look, call the hospital, call another doctor. There're other ways to take care of a bun in the oven. And don't dwell on what happened this afternoon. Obviously the guy's a real shit who ought to be turned in, and maybe you'll want to do that. But right now you solve the baby problem, then you think about what else you want to do."

"Okay," she said. And she smiled a little, and we got back in the cab, me in front and her in back.

So, like I said, I thought she was going to be all right. She didn't say anything while we drove down past the big houses and then down the hill toward where she lived. But I thought she was okay.

The light was red at the bottom where Victoria Street crosses Sherbrooke. The streetlights had come on too: it was only 5:30 but we still were a long way from the real change in seasons. I would have continued and then turned down her street to take her home, but while we waited for the light to change she reached forward and tapped me on the shoulder.

"Thanks," she said. "How much do I owe you? I'll get out here and walk the rest of the way, it'll do me good."

I looked up at her in the rear-view. She didn't look too bad, she was even trying to smile a little. "Hey, forget about the fare. When you've got some super job somewhere or you've won the Lotto you can pay me double."

"Or when I marry some rich man?" she said, still digging in her purse.

"I didn't say that," I said.

She left her hand on my shoulder for a second. "I appreciate that," she said. "I *will* pay you double some day, but take the $5 now."

She got out of the cab. The light changed for me just then, and I turned right. She waved as I went passed.

It was a couple of seconds before I looked in my rear-view again to see what she was doing. Just at the right moment. Just as she stepped in front of the bus that came barrelling through the intersection trying to make the light.

The fur coat was covered in blood when I got back to her. The same colour as her lipstick.

Nothing But Good Times

Sylvie was thinking about what she should wear that night when the old woman started waving the $5 bill in her face. She'd already gone on to the next customer, pushing his things through so she could start ringing them up. When she looked around, she was surprised to see the old woman was still there.

"Give me another bill. This one is torn," the woman said. She had to be old even though her skin, the colour of weak tea, was practically unlined. Her hair, which showed around the beret pulled down on her head, was black with a strong sprinkling of white. Her body was shapeless: the breasts seemed to have melted down toward her waist. Her shopping-bags still sat on the counter, just where Sylvie was supposed to put the next person's groceries.

"I want another bill," the woman said. "This one is bad, don't you see, girl?"

Sylvie didn't reply. A bill was a bill, and besides she had other things to worry about. She'd left a few clothes at Anthony's but it was Saturday afternoon and his mother would be there. To change at his place would open up all sorts of things that Sylvie didn't want to have to deal with.

"I want another bill," the woman said again.

Last weekend, Easter weekend they spent at the Mirabel Hilton, out by the airport. Nice place. They had a room that overlooked the indoor garden and the swimming pool and they'd swum and drunk and made love and smoked a little dope. Couldn't expect to do something like that this weekend but Anthony usually had good ideas....

The man next in line shifted his weight and began to pull his wallet out of his pocket. Sylvie jabbed at the cash register with her right hand while she moved the items with her left. There were no bar code readers here, no carousels to push groceries past the cashier. This was your basic centre-city store: crowded, sometimes dirty, definitely not state-of-the-art.

And not the store where Sylvie would have chosen to work. If she hadn't met Anthony she would have quit after the first month. But he was fun and he worked up the street at the hardware store. He had a car, a red TransAm. He dressed sharp. He liked to have a good time. A good time, that's what he'd promised her for tonight too....

The old woman leaned her belly against the counter and waved the bill so Sylvie couldn't miss it. "You trying to cheat me, girl."

The man next in line laughed "Oh, give her a new bill," he said. "She'll stand there all afternoon if you don't."

Sylvie looked up at him: grey hair and beard, dark green leather jacket. He had money, he probably never worked in a place like this. She shrugged and continued to ring up his things.

"She'll change it," the man said to the old woman. "Just wait a second."

The woman spun around so she could stare at the man. She looked him up and down. "What makes you think so? They're all alike," she said. She smoothed the bill again in her hand. "All alike, wanting to do dirty to the rest of us."

Sylvie decided she didn't need this five minutes before her break, five minutes before Anthony was supposed to meet her. She punched in the code that opened the cash drawer and very carefully chose a fresh bill from among the ones in the $5 compartment. She smoothed it, held it up to the light as if to check its honesty and then held it out to the old woman with a bow.

The old woman grabbed the new bill and wadded the old one up in a ball before throwing it at the girl.

"Oh, shit," Sylvie said to herself. But the old woman heard her.

"Watch your tongue, girl," the woman shouted "God gave us language." The woman's voice was strong but her rage and her accent made her English hard to follow. "Language is a gift from God, and you shouldn't go messing with it, saying bad things and all."

Sylvie didn't say anything. She started to put the man's groceries in shopping-bags.

The old woman looked at her but didn't move. "Language is gift of God, and man shouldn't trifle with it," she shouted. "Read your scripture. Do you hear me, girl?"

The man laughed, still holding out his money.

The woman, however, looked even angrier. She turned so she could look at all the people standing in line, waiting to pay for their Saturday shopping. "Read your scripture," she shouted. "All of you: read your scripture and lead a Godly life." She waited a moment, as if expecting a shout of affirmation from the waiting people. But when it didn't come, she hoisted her shopping-bags and began to lurch toward the door.

Sylvie took the man's money. She saw that he smiled at her conspiratorially. "We're all going to get old one day," he said, "but I hope I don't get like that."

She nodded, but what he said didn't really register. She could see Anthony already in her imagination: his white teeth, his curly black hair, his neat little moustache, the gold stud in his left ear lobe. He'd be wearing his red sweater over a white shirt with the blue and red striped tie, loosened a little. His black leather coat too, with the red scarf tucked in the top. She loved to see him hurrying down the street from the hardware store, rolling slightly as he walked, full of life, promising excitement.

When she came out of the store, he was already waiting for her, smoking a cigarette and laughing about something. She started to run toward him, and she only saw the woman out of the corner of her eye. It took her several moments before she realized what he was laughing at.

"Look at that old fool," he said, pointing toward the old woman. She had made it as far as the bus stop at the corner of Park and St. Viateur. Her shopping-bags sat on the pavement beside her, and three teenagers were sitting on the wall across from her.

The handle had torn off one of the bags, and she was talking. They couldn't hear her words, but Sylvie could imagine. "Language is a gift from God. Read your scripture."

The boys laughed. "Memère," one of them shouted, loud enough to be heard over the traffic, "there is no God."

The tallest boy jumped down from the wall and came over to stand beside the woman. He said something and his friends laughed. His hands were in his pockets, but he held his elbows out like a bird on the attack who fluffs his feathers to look bigger.

Probably nothing would have happened then, but who knows? The 80 bus arrived, the boys got on, Anthony hustled Sylvie inside the restaurant. The woman must have continued home. Sylvie never even wondered.

About the only thing she wondered about during that time was whether this was love. Certainly that night he said he loved her, and she knew that her thoughts returned again and again to him. She knew that during the week, when she saw him pass in front of the store, adrenalin shot through her hands and the tips of her breasts tightened. She suspected that he had things to show her that she would never learn from anyone else. She could pick his voice out of the hodge-podge of sound in the hardware store. She could even tell his car when it drove up her street.

She would look at herself in the mirror and think that if it wasn't love, then it would do for now.

Spring was late that year. By the middle of April piles of snow still lay rutted in the lanes and packed under stairways, but they went for rides in his car with all the windows rolled down anyway. The air sometimes smelled damp and faintly of green. Other times what Sylvie smelled when she waited for him to meet her was dog droppings and garbage now uncovered after months of being hidden by the snow.

By then Anthony thought they ought to move in together; his mother was moving to a smaller apartment now that it was clear that his father was gone for good. That meant there wouldn't be as much room for him. But if Sylvie and he put their resources together they could get a nice place in this neighbourhood or practically any other, he said. They were made for each other, he'd add. Then he would put his arms around her, reaching inside her coat if they were outside, running his hands over her back and sides, wherever they were. She found that difficult to argue with.

But she knew her parents would protest when she said she wanted to move out. Not that Anthony's mother liked her, either. But it didn't matter. She decided that when she wasn't around him she was only half alive. Even the way he'd started borrowing from her didn't bother her. After all, he'd paid for all their good times up until then; it was only fair, she told herself, that she start paying some too.

But he was late meeting her at the souvlaki place on the last Friday afternoon in April. He should have gotten off work 45 minutes before, and even figuring that he stopped by the bank to cash his pay cheque, he should have come by now. She looked at her watch again and looked out the window of the restaurant. The setting sun coloured the sky above the buildings across the street. The days were getting longer. If they were going to take a place, the next few weeks would be the time to go looking, because leases were coming due all over the town.

There was a place for rent across the street: one of the

duplexes that had been done over. She wanted something new, though, she wanted something that had some of the flash and glamour of the Mirabel Hilton. She didn't want something renovated, she wanted something shiny. Otherwise she might as well stay home.

Then the crazy old woman came past, dragging a shopping-cart behind her. The cart was loaded and Sylvie was glad she hadn't been working when the old bitch came through the checkout. For just an instant their eyes met but Sylvie looked away quickly. The old woman continued down the street to the first of the row of three-storey triplexes where she stopped and sat down on the steps.

No. Sylvie didn't want to live in this neighbourhood.

And where was Anthony?

There, coming out of the bank, cutting across the street against the light, dodging a taxi. His jacket was open and his scarf was flying behind him. She felt her heart jump, and fingers tingle. She'd never known anyone who made her feel the way he did.

He saw her through the window, and blew her a kiss as he passed. In three seconds he was standing beside her, leaning over, kissing her, pressing his cold cheek against her warm one. But he didn't sit down.

"Listen, Angel," he said, kneeling beside the table so their faces were on the same level. He held her right hand in his left, leaving her left hand free to rest lightly around the back of his neck. He looked in her eyes. His breath was warm on her face. She wanted to be alone with him as soon as possible.

"Yes," she said expectantly.

He swallowed before he started to speak. "Listen, I got to run."

She clutched at his hand. "Hey, no, you can't do that. We were going to go out to dinner," she said. She felt the anger rise up inside her. Damn it, she'd been waiting. Why

42

did he have to run out?

He reached over so he could give her a little kiss on the cheek. "It's all right, Angel, not to worry. All I've got to do is go around the corner and see this guy."

"Why?" she asked. There was something more behind this too, she suddenly suspected. He looked, what? Upset?

"Why?" he asked back. His gaze went out the window as if he were seeking the answer there. Then obviously he decided he had to tell her something. "I got to see a guy about the car repairs."

"There's something wrong with the car? It was okay last weekend."

He hesitated. Then he stood up, and leaned over to kiss her again. "It's nothing to worry about," he said. "Look, I'll be back in fifteen minutes. You stay here, order us both a beer and some Greek salad or something and when I come back we'll decide where to go."

"Hey, no," she said. "Come back. Don't run out on me." But he was wrapping his scarf around his neck, and opening the outside door.

Fifteen minutes. His fifteen minutes was usually longer than that, but then he'd never left her in the lurch like that before either. Maybe he really only had to do something about the car. She hoped, she hoped. The waitress came over to see if she wanted to order. For a second Sylvie though about nursing her coffee a while longer, but then she decided, what the heck. She ordered fries and two beers. If Anthony didn't come back quickly, she'd drink the second one too.

He said around the corner. He said car repairs. He hadn't mentioned anything about that until then. But she hadn't seen him driving to work, either, and he hadn't said anything about going any place in it on the weekend. Maybe there was something wrong. But why hadn't he mentioned it before?

43

He had secrets, that she knew. But then so did she. Secrets were normal. You couldn't let them get in the way. Life was too short, there wasn't enough fun in it to ruin what there was by worry. That's what he'd showed her. That's what he always said: good times, we're going to have nothing but good times.

The old woman was getting up. She grabbed hold of the handles of the shopping-cart. She turned it around so that it was easier to pull, then she started down the street again, her head thrown back. She was singing, Sylvie suspected, although Sylvie could hear nothing.

It was getting darker now, the streetlights came on. From two of the houses on this side of the street, black-coated Hasidic men came out followed by a gaggle of small boys. The old woman stopped and watched them. She was saying something about Jesus, Sylvie imagined. She wondered what the Hasidic men thought about that.

The waitress came over with the fries and the beers. Sylvie took a few tentative sips of her beer as she watched the old woman open the little metal gate that enclosed the patch of front yard and then wrestle the cart around the stairs which led to the second floor. It was hard to tell from a distance but Sylvie guessed she must live in a basement apartment that had a separate entrance, down a few steps from the sidewalk level.

The woman must have opened the door. An outside light flooded the little front yard and an ordinary light appeared in the window. Sylvie allowed herself to wonder what it was like inside the apartment; pictures of Jesus, crocheted afghans, postcards from the Rockies and the CN Tower. A cat or two maybe; she tried to remember if the old lady bought cat food.

But suddenly the woman appeared again, as if she'd been thrown up the stairs by something. She stood for a second on the sidewalk and then threw back her head and arms in a scream that Sylvie could almost hear.

Two Hasidic boys turned around to stare at her, and then hurried on. A woman on a bicycle pulled to a stop just past her, however. The old woman didn't see her coming because her body was still contorted in the scream.

Jesus Christ, Sylvie thought, what the hell is going on now?

The bicycle woman looked around her, as if wondering what was needed, who could help. She apparently saw the door open to the basement apartment and left the old woman standing to go look inside. Then she came hurrying out too. But instead of screaming she went and pounded on the doors to the apartments on the first floor.

No-one answered. The woman ran up the outside stairs to the second floor, where she pounded on the doors there. She was about ready to head for the third floor when the left-hand door on the bottom opened.

Sylvie, of course, could not hear what was being said, but she could tell from the way the man at the door reacted that something grave had happened. He turned around and headed back into the apartment, leaving the door open. The woman stood watching for a moment, before she ran down the stairs to the old woman. There she tried to get the old one to sit down on the steps.

Sylvie looked at her watch; it had been 25 minutes since Anthony left. She felt a little shiver run down her back: not fear exactly but a sort of worried questioning. Just around the corner, he had said. Then she heard the sirens. One siren—a police car—turned off the avenue and roared by the restaurant. It turned the wrong way down the one-way street. A yellow 911 van followed.

Sylvie stood up. The two waitresses were looking out the window and a handful of people had already stopped at the corner to look down the street. Another police car drove up, this one without its siren running. The 911 squad pushed past the old woman. One of the policemen with a clipboard began to ask questions of the other people who lived in the building.

The old woman watched, but nobody asked her anything. She tried to move back toward her apartment, but one of the policemen stood in her way. She said something, but the man shook his head.

Sylvie watched and waited for the explosion. But the old woman just stood there, as if what was happening was completely beyond her. A medic hurried past to the emergency van and came back with a gurney. Another 911 car drove up, a third police car swung into place at the far end of the block to keep traffic from turning onto the street.

Then slowly the woman started to walk up the street. She held both fists to her head, and her eyes seemed focused on the pavement in front of her. She walked slowly, she seemed to be unaware of the people watching what was going on. She was talking to herself, Sylvie saw. She was in a world apart.

The man who owned the restaurant came out from the kitchen and saw the waitresses staring out the window. "Hey," he yelled. "There's work to be done:" One of the waitresses tried to explain what was going on. "I don't care if there's a Jesus Christ himself being crucified in the next block," he said. "As long as it's not in here, and it's working hours, we've got to work."

But he came over to the window to look too. He stood beside Sylvie's table and peered down the street. "Ha, looks like it's the Shark's place,' he said. "Somebody must have got it."

"The shark?" Sylvie heard herself repeating.

"Yeah, that's not his name, but he's a loan shark. Rough customer. Does a little small-time dealing too," he said. He turned around to look at Sylvie. "A place to stay away from, Miss."

46

Sylvie shivered. The other clerks at the store still talked about the time a year ago when there were a couple of shooting galleries on Park Avenue. Didn't last long, the cops cleaned them out after about three months. But while they were there the store had a steady stream of half-stoned people buying soft drinks and packaged cakes. Weird people with needle tracks on their hands and, sometimes, wildness in their eyes.

They'd been gone before Sylvie started working there. That didn't mean there weren't other strange things going on, though.

Sylvie took a big drink of her beer. Her stomach tightened as the cold liquid ran inside her. She wished that Anthony would show up so they could go some place else. He always said he had nothing but contempt for people who used drugs. He knew some, who didn't after all? But aside from a joint now and then, to celebrate something, he always said he was proud to be clean. He wouldn't have anything to do with somebody who was dealing.

But then Sylvie became aware of eyes on her and she turned to look out the window. The old woman was there, staring at her. Then she reached up and rapped on the window with both her fists. "Your man," she shouted loud enough to be heard through the glass. "The wages of sin are death. Your man has been paid in full."

Anthony. The car repairs. The Shark. Sylvie stood up quickly, almost knocking over her chair and the beer. She grabbed for her coat and her purse. The waitress saw her and started toward her. "You haven't paid," she said.

Sylvie stopped and rummaged in the purse. She found first a handful of change but she knew that wouldn't be enough. Then she found a $10 bill: too much, not enough? She didn't know, but it would have to do. As she hurried out the door, she thrust it at the waitress.

Outside the damp cold hit her in the face. The old

woman was there at the corner, her hands covering her face and her body rocking from side to side. Sylvie stopped in front of her: "What did you say?" she asked, reaching out to take the woman by her shoulders to shake her.

The woman looked up. Her face was grey, her eyes were bloodshot. "Your man," she said, "and the other. The Lord has acted."

She would have continued, but Sylvie started to run down the street. One of the policemen was in a patrol car, talking on the radio, two others were on the second floor landing, talking to the people who lived there. The medics were still bent over by the entrance to the basement apartment. Sylvie stopped when she got to them.

By then she knew what to expect. It was Anthony all right, lying curled on his left side, his right arm up over his head as if protecting it. There was a line of blood running out of his mouth. His eyes were shut, his skin was pale under the stubble of whiskers. The red scarf was still around his neck, pulled tight, but Sylvie also saw the smooth curve of his forehead was broken. The skin appeared uncut but the bone underneath it was pushed in. He was breathing, she could see his chest moving underneath the blanket which covered him from his shoulders to his feet.

"Anthony," she said, softly.

One of the medics heard and turned around. "You know him?" he asked.

She nodded.

The medic stood up. "He'll be all right probably.'

"Oh," she said. She took a step closer. She was shivering, she realized. Car repairs he'd said. Being beaten up had nothing to do with car repairs. "He was mugged," she said. Anybody could be mugged. It happened all the time.

"Maybe, maybe not," the medic said. "You should talk to the police about that."

Which meant, what? That it didn't look like a simple

urban crime, the innocent assaulted by the wicked. How could she tell, how could they tell?

"God will have his way," came the old woman's voice from the doorway. She must have followed Sylvie back to the scene. Or perhaps she had merely come home: her shopping-cart still stood in the open doorway. "He dared to mess with the ungodly, and the ungodly smote him. Let that be a lesson to you, girl. Avoid evil, and the appearance of evil. Live cleanly, act justly, cast the devils from you...."

Sylvie shut her eyes. They ought to call Anthony's mother, she'd want to know what had happened. They'd have to talk to his boss too. They'd want to know what he'd been doing, where he was going. There were a lot of questions that were going to have to be answered.

"Who hit him?" she asked. "He left me just a couple of minutes ago, who ever hit him can't be very far away."

"Did he have any enemies?" one of the policemen asked, coming over with a clipboard. "Do you know if he was in any trouble?"

"Who hit him?" she asked again. "Does he have any money on him? He'd just gone to the bank, he should have quite a bit even if he did pay somebody...."

The policeman looked interested, but before he could question her back, the door at the rear of the basement opened, a door which looked as if it went to the trash containers or the furnace-room. Sylvie held her breath as soon as she heard the hinges begin to move. The eyes that peeked through the narrow crack were dark and suspicious, and when the policeman ordered the door opened further, they blinked twice, as if considering.

"No," Sylvie said out loud.

A tiny groan came from Anthony, so tiny that Sylvie could barely hear it. She wanted to lean over, to listen more closely, but the sight of the eyes at the door made her blood freeze. This could not be happening. All she wanted was a

49

good time, she hadn't asked for anything more than that. Surely people were allowed to enjoy themselves. Why this?

The groan thickened into a sort of croak in the back of Anthony's throat. The medic who'd been monitoring his blood pressure looked up and called something to his colleague that Sylvie didn't catch. The policeman stepped forward and put his hand gently on the her arm. "Miss," he began.

But she knew she couldn't stay any longer even before the medics began to push her out of the way. He was mugged, she told herself again. Of course that's what happened. This isn't a safe place to work, or even to be.

"A very shady character," said somebody in the crowd which was gathering by the outside door.

"Thought he'd moved out, we'd been given assurances..." somebody else said.

"Guy was a clerk at the hardware store, saw him come around once or twice before."

"Shark."

"In over his head...."

Sylvie was at the door now. She wanted out. She would leave and never come back. She didn't belong here, nobody belonged here.

"You can't leave," the old woman said, as she started down the walkway toward the street. "The Lord will judge you, you have to wait...." The red car, Anthony's red car, was parked half-way down the block. Sylvie brushed past the old woman's hand, held out to detain her. If she got to the car, everything would be all right. Anthony would get well, the world would go on, there would be pleasure again.

But before she got there, she heard the old woman screaming: "She's going, she's going. You cannot let her get away."

And then she knew she was trapped, and that it would be a long time before the next good time.

2
Getting By

Frances and Daniel

Let me tell you about the couple in the van. I don't want to talk about that other business, and you'd find it boring, I expect. It happened a long time ago, and while you might listen for a while now, after a few minutes you'd fidget, and you'd say, Frances, let's talk about something else. Besides, the longer it lies there in the background, the better. I do not want to have to wrestle it down again. I like being able to think about other things.

So I will tell you about the couple instead. I noticed the van the morning after the leaves fell. During the night the wind had raced through, tearing them from the trees. The van might have been there earlier, but it was a difficult fall, as I said, and for several weeks I ran the two-mile track around the neighbourhood each morning in a fog.

That morning, though, the brilliance of the sky shook me out of my self. The air was full of the rich, fresh smell of leaves, and I could see the sun shining already on the top of Mount Royal.

The van was parked at the corner just before the park: a blue Dodge with no lettering to indicate who owned it. Curtains were pulled around the windows in the back, so I thought: refugees from the sixties or seventies, road people just passing through. I turned my head as I passed to see the licence plate, wondering how travellers would end up so far from the main routes through Montreal.

The van had local plates, though, and just as I was turning back to look where I was going, a man's head appeared. Dark skin, straight black hair, straight nose: East Indian I guessed. A second later a woman sat up, and I was sure. She was very pretty, with dark hair parted in the middle and pulled back to form a frame for her face with its big black eyes, her full, smiling mouth. For a second I looked at them looking at each other, and I felt a little of the energy that passed between them. Then, embarrassed at my intrusion into their lives, I ran across the street and into my own life.

Which, I see now, wasn't so terrible. You'd probably laugh if I told you. Whatever, I didn't notice the van again for a week. Then, one morning the van was parked where I'd seen it before and the couple were in each other's arms. Interesting, I remember thinking.

The Tuesday afterwards the van was there again. It was cold and I saw with a start of understanding that, aha, the windows were steamed up.

So, I thought to myself, as I continued running down the street. So that is what they are doing.

But why in the van? This was a period, I must tell you, when I spent a good deal of time imagining scenes of passion, and I found myself wondering what it would be like in the back of the van. Did the man use it during the day for deliveries, did they push aside his tool box and spread a blanket or a sleeping-bag in the free space? And I wondered: was there something clandestine about them? Was she married to somebody else? Did they love each other despairingly, impossibly, against the wishes of everyone in their families? She was so young, though, and they were there so often, that in the end I decided they must have the right to be together.

And then I tried to imagine what it must be like where they lived. In an apartment, sharing with his brother, the brother's wife, and their two children, maybe. Or with her mother and father and sisters. Where everyone heard every noise. And I remembered a week spent with Daniel's parents where we had slept next to each other without touching because every movement could be heard by his little sister in the room next door.

So they must leave the apartment when the others were just beginning to stir. They must go out in the thin light of

dawn into the van, the one place to have an hour by themselves before she climbed the stairs in the garment factory a
mile farther east along this street. And so she would sit at
the sewing-machine after making love, with flesh still
singing, with a memory of the beloved's eyes upon her,
with the feel of his hands and his weight and his tongue.
Going to work, too, one must add, without a chance to
wash.

As I said, passion concerned me then, and I began to look
for them every morning I ran. When I saw them I smiled to
myself.

October is a fine month, but in French they rightly call
November *le mois des morts*, the month of the dead. It rains a
lot, the sky is grey, and the leaves that haven't been swept
up lie rotting in the gutters. I say I don't mind running
when it rains, but it's easier to find excuses when the
weather's bad: breakfast meetings which mean you've got to
get out of the house early. Sick kids, who need more attention than usual even though they're pretty big. Colds that
suggest you, yourself, shouldn't get over-tired. Then comes
the morning when you look out and see the first snow
falling: three inches already and neither have the streets
been salted nor have the sidewalk tractors passed to clear
the way. Running would clearly be foolish.

So I didn't go out as often then and I didn't see the van
as often. It was there, though, when I did run. The windows were steamy usually, and once, toward the end of
November when I was later than usual, I saw the man wiping the inside of the windshield. She sat beside him, brushing her hair and smiling. I doubt whether they ever noticed
me.

I never asked Daniel if he had seen them when he ran.
We were not talking about love much at that point. Not
that we were fighting much either. It was as if we both
were afraid what might happen if we talked too much, as if

54

we both knew of my secrets and his suspicions and neither wanted to bring them out into the light. But I wondered about the young couple constantly.

Then about 4:30 one afternoon in early December I found myself near the garment factories: it's not important to say why, except that I had promised to pick up a package for a friend. I stood on the corner of St. Lawrence and St. Viateur with my arms full, trying to hail a cab. The sun had already set, yesterday's snow had turned to black slush, my feet were wet, and no taxi driver seemed to understand what I wanted. Then I saw the van across the street. He was there on the sidewalk, standing by the van, arms folded, looking east down the street.

The doors of the building across the street opened and three women hurried out, pulling on tuques, looking quickly eastward to see if the bus were coming from that way. Behind them other women hurried out, some of them sticking their hands in their pockets and turning bravely west to face the wind and a walk home. Others walked just as quickly to the corner and stopped to wait for the next bus north to inch its way up St. Lawrence. Then came a gaggle of younger women, laughing as they stepped outside, and looking up, then down the street. I remember coming out of places like that, work over, nothing pressing, sure that something interesting would happen now. Sometimes Daniel would be there, and when I saw him I couldn't stop smiling. I tried to sometimes, because, you know, I didn't want him to know I cared so much. But I did, and he did and for a while we were very happy. He is a fine person, no doubt about it: I have told myself often just what a fine person he is and how one does not hurt people like that.

But being on time matters to him, and I cannot imagine him waiting for me for very long, even if it were he who arrived ahead of time. If he did, at the very least, he would be in a black humour.

55

The young man was not. When the door to the only factory in this block opened he quit slouching and stood up straighter. She was not in the first group to come out. But when she did, his face lit up. She saw him almost immediately and came hurrying toward him. They did not touch but smiled at each other when he opened the door to the van for her.

I watched until the van was gone, and then I slogged on to deliver the package.

Now I wonder what would have happened if I had told my friend about the couple. I was surprised to find him there; he'd gone to Ottawa months before, he was just back to get something from the people he'd sublet to. He took the package, and thanked me, and then, because we had already agreed there would be no more, I turned and went down the stairs. When I got down to the street I cried. As I said, though, I do not really want to talk about all that.

Christmas came and went. The kids were both in school programs. Daniel's mother was here for the holiday. We went skiing twice. I didn't run again until the middle of January.

And then the van wasn't there. Not surprising, of course. It was the dead of winter. But as I watched the sidewalk in front of me carefully to avoid icy patches, I wondered what they were doing now. Maybe they'd been able to get a place by themselves. If both of them were working they probably would be able to swing it, unless they were helping support the rest of the family.

Family: I thought as I rounded the park. It had to be an arranged marriage, or at least the parents must have approved it. Had they discovered each other on their own? Or was that passion something they found afterwards, in the darkness, alone?

I shivered, and not because of the wind coming straight at me down the street.

Winter is hard on people. Even the young and the strong don't venture out as much. You can go for months without seeing neighbours you see daily during the summer. For the old, ice on the sidewalks can imprison just as surely bars.

It was about this time that Mrs. Burke, the woman who lived across the street, fell on the walkway in front of her house. Daniel saw her, when he was coming home in the middle of the day to pick up a report he'd forgotten. Good thing: the street was deserted.

If she hadn't been injured he would have hauled her to her feet and helped her back in the house. But when he hurried over she began to cry. He put his hands under her arms and tried to sit her up, but she bit her lip and tears streamed from her eyes.

"No," she whispered to him. "No, don't move me. There's something the matter." So he held her hand until the ambulance came. "Don't tell Ray," she told him when they waited in the emergency-room. "Don't tell him I was outside. He doesn't like me to go outside in this kind of weather."

We knew that: we had heard them arguing early in the morning when she would go out to the get the paper, and he would be right behind her, yelling. She would yell back, and I would lie in bed, listening to them until she would stomp back inside, and he would follow, slamming the door after him.

He yelled at her in the emergency-room too. Screamed, called her a stupid broad. She turned her head away from him, brought her hand up to cover her eyes, and cried quietly. Finally when he paused for breath she put out her other hand to touch his arm. "Ray, Ray," she said. "Stop it. You're going to have a heart attack, and then where will we be?"

Daniel laughed when he told me. I laughed too. What else can you do?

Mrs. Burke was in the hospital for a long time. They put a pin her leg, and the wound didn't heal properly, and then she had to go to a convalescent place for physiotherapy. Mr. Burke wanted to stay at home by himself but his son's wife insisted he come to their house. Otherwise, she told one of the other neighbours, he wouldn't eat, just drink.

By then the weather was getting better. Still cold, still slippery on many mornings, but the sky was pale at 7 AM and the wind did not cut so. My friend called me once, in the afternoon when he expected Daniel not to be there. Daniel was home sick though, and he answered the phone on the extension by the bed before I made it to the one in the kitchen. I listened to the silence before my friend said: "Excuse me, I've made a mistake." Then he hung up, and I found my hands making mistakes all afternoon. But I won't go into that.

No, I will tell you about running on spring mornings. Sometime in April when the snow is gone and the earth has grown soft enough for the worms to crawl out of their dungeons, you hear robins singing as the sky turns pink in the east. That year by springtime I could leave the house and think about something other than my problems.

The first really warm morning Daniel had to go to Ottawa and I did not have to be at work until noon. I started out on my usual track but the air smelled of tulips and the tiny yellow blossoms of the maples. I reached the farthest point and suddenly I realized I wasn't tired, so instead of turning back I went on, I went west.

Then at a big intersection I had to stop for a red light. I ran in place looking at the apartment blocks. Three storeys high, most of them, built in the immediate post-war period. Mostly in good repair, but only because rental housing has been at such a premium in our city. That was when I saw the Indian couple coming out of the apartment building on my left.

58

They did not look at each other as they walked down the front walk and out to the street. He went ahead, directly to the van which was parked in front. She moved heavily, shuffling along, one hand clutching a purse, the other pressed against the side of her big, pregnant belly. He was in the car with the ignition switched on before she made it around to the passenger side. She stood for a moment looking up and down the street, waiting for him to unlock the door. When he didn't, she tapped on the window. He didn't turn immediately: the engine was running rough and obviously he was listening to what was wrong.

She tapped louder. He looked up, and when he reached over to open the door, she began to yell at him. He yelled back.

Even though I didn't understand the language, I understood the tone. The words probably didn't matter even to them. What was important was the disappointment, the fatigue, the problems that they were facing. For the moment, the magic they found in each other was gone. As they drove off, each hunched against a door, I wondered if they would ever find it again.

Magic. Well, if not magic there was some luck in the fact that I made it home. I don't remember turning back, and I couldn't tell you what route I took. I kept running until the corner before our place and I was still breathing hard when Mr. Burke stopped me.

"She's dead," he said.

I'm afraid I looked at him blankly, without even recognizing him. I was suddenly aware that I was home, that I smelled of sweat, that something terrible had happened to this man.

"What?" I said, resisting the impulse to reach out and touch him. Behind him I suddenly saw his son.

"Mother died this morning. Pneumonia," the son said. I must have looked shocked although I couldn't think of anything to do except mumble a few words.

"She shouldn't have done it, you know. She should never have gone outside. It wasn't safe. She knew it," Mr. Burke said. "She knew how dangerous it was." He looked much smaller than he had before, as if he were a blow-up toy that had a slow leak in it. His wrinkles were more pronounced, his bluster was gone.

Daniel didn't get back until late, until the kids were ready for bed. He said goodnight to them and then stood looking through the mail while I told him about Mrs. Burke.

"What?" he said, looking up, as if he just realized I was talking to him. He had a magazine which had come that day open in his hand. His eyes were red from his contact lenses.

"I was talking about Mrs. Burke: I said her husband is insisting on a big show...."

"Oh," he said. "Too bad." He turned the page in the magazine.

I stared at him. He didn't seem to care, and that wasn't like him. He was kind. Whatever else I might think about him—had thought about him—his kindness was always there like a backdrop, the given against which I had to consider everything else about him. I didn't say anything for a moment, because then he went on. "I saw that friend of yours," he said. "Forget his name, the guy who went to work for that consulting firm. Said to say hello."

I sucked in my breath and looked at him. For a moment our eyes met, and I guessed at just how much he knew, just how much he had known, and why he couldn't care about Mrs. Burke right then. But I was not going to throw whatever it was we had away. Not after I had fought to keep things afloat for so long. "Oh," I said. "Nice of him. Do you want something to eat?"

It was warm enough that night that we left all the windows open, and the warm smell of growing things came in with the sounds of the night. We watched the late news in bed, and then Daniel read the newspaper. I turned the light off on my side and lay thinking about what else to say, about the Indian couple, about my friend. After half an hour, Daniel finished and dropped the newspaper on the floor and turned off the light. I could feel him looking at me in the darkness, but after a moment he turned over to face in the other direction. For a long time afterwards I lay, not daring to move, listening.

A breeze came up and blew the curtain, rustling it against the ferns on the window-sill. A couple walked by not saying anything, their footsteps echoing against the houses. And Daniel breathed carefully, deeply but not quite asleep.

Then a car pulled up and we heard Mr. Burke get out: "Thank you, my boy," he said loudly. "No, no, keep the change. There's plenty more where that came from."

The taxi driver said something too softly to be understood.

"No, no," Mr. Burke said. "That'll be all right. I've got my key right here. I'll be all right." And the taxi door slammed and his footsteps went up the steps while the taxi drove off down the street.

I felt my muscles tense: I knew what was going to happen. First you would hear him rummaging, scrabbling around on the porch while he tried to fit the key into the lock. Then when he couldn't get it in, he would tap on the glass part of the door with keys. Finally he would begin to yell for Mrs. Burke. Several times, I had watched from our window as she came out in her dressing-gown, scolding him to get in here, asking him when he was ever going to learn, if he wanted to wake the dead. She would glance up nervously at the windows in the houses around: embarrassed I imagined. Then she had him drape his arm around her shoulder and she led him back in the house.

This time she wasn't there of course.

I listened to him struggle, bracing myself for the moment when he started to yell. "Rita," he called. "Rita, come let me in."

Daniel jerked awake and sat up. "What's he up to?" he asked.

"Drunk," I said. "Drunk enough so he doesn't remember."

Daniel was up now, looking out the window.

"Rita," Mr. Burke shouted. "Rita, can you hear me?"

"Can't let him go on like that," Daniel said. He turned and started to pull on his trousers.

"Rita, I want you," the old man was yelling. "Rita."

Then the memory must have burst suddenly on the old man because his shouts dissolved in tears. You could hear the great heart-wrenching sobs as if he were beside you.

Daniel went over to look out the window again. "Well, if he didn't drop the key, I can probably get the door open for him. That'll let him in the house at least."

I took up his place by the window and watched while he went out, crossed the street, and talked the old man into letting him open the door. He was inside the house for a good ten minutes, and when he came back he sat for several minutes on the edge of the bed before he began to take off his clothes again.

I said nothing, but I wondered what he would do if I put out my hand, palm flat, and ran it down his back. It had been a long time since I had done that; for months and months he had been the one who had started things. When anything was started.

Finally, he said; "Did you love him a lot?"

He wasn't talking about Mr. Burke for sure. But it was a fair question. Oh yes, I loved him. For ages, I awoke in the morning to thoughts of him, I made love to him in Daniel's body, I was mad for him. But why? I don't know. Probably for reasons you wouldn't want to talk about, that you'd laugh at if you could uncover. Which was why it had to end. The good reasons were on the other side.

"It's over," I said. "Has been for a while."

He turned so he could look at me. "That doesn't answer my question."

"It's the only answer I can give," I said. Then I hesitated because what I was going to say next might change everything. "Any other might hurt too much. Take it or leave it."

He shut his eyes, but didn't say anything.

I waited. Then I sat up so I could put out my hand, the way I used to, back when we had first discovered each other. I let it fall lightly on his shoulder and then I ran it down the shoulder-blade to his side so I could pass it around his waist and rest myself against his back, my face against his other shoulder. For a second I sat like that, listening to him breathe. The breeze stirred the curtain again, the sidewalk outside was empty.

"Don't leave me," he said, as he turned so he could put his arms around me. "I don't want to be alone."

I moved so I fit better in his arms. "Don't worry," I said, thinking of the Burkes, thinking of the Indian couple, thinking of the boring story you wouldn't want to hear. "I don't either."

63

Flood Damage

It is nearly midnight, but Brent still is watching the flood coverage on CNN. Too late for an six year old but 1) it is too hot to sleep and 2) the social worker said it's probably good for him.

She also said it probably was good for Anne to make lists of what she had to do. Good for organization, she said: it would make Anne feel like she was accomplishing something. Anne thought it was evidence of just how little the social worker knew.

The floods on television bear no comparison to their flood. Those floods have been going on for days now: the satellite pictures of the mass of water, the lines of people filling sandbags, the bulldozers trying to keep the levees in place.

Their flood was different. To see that, all you've got to do is look at the videos that Anne's mother made of the news coverage. Anne does, sometimes after Brent has finally fallen asleep. The part Anne likes best is where the helicopter rescues the woman. But Anne can't watch it when Brent is around. Not yet, the social worker says. Maybe later, when he's healed.

Healed! He's okay, to look at him. So is Jerry. Maybe Anne is too.

Out there on the river, though, what she regretted most was how mad she'd been. "Go," she'd told Jerry when they got the wet sweaters and sleeping-bags and jackets loaded into the dryers at the laundromat. "Go, get out of here, leave me in peace." She was damn glad to see them head down to the river.

It had been raining since the night before even though it was supposed to be a drought year. But then Anne supposed that was par for the course; the trip was supposed to be a wilderness adventure, after all. Good for them. Cheap because Jerry'd been out of work so long. Fun because they'd been through such tough times.

It was the rain in the forecast that made Jerry think he could get away with a campfire. Because of the drought, every place they camped handed out these notices: no open fires.

But Jerry said with the rain coming and seeing how it was their last night before they headed home, a small fire wouldn't hurt. "Got to give the kid the whole experience. It'll be okay, don't worry. Trust me."

So Anne caved in once again, and there'd she'd been, trying to wash dishes on the picnic table, with the thunder already beginning in the distance. And then all of sudden Brent was squealing. "Hey, look, a sparkler."

She turned around just in time to see him waving the stick with the flaming marshmallow. The flame arched through the sky like a Roman candle, leaving a trail of sparks, but it couldn't do too much damage because it was going to fall well away from the tent or....

But she was wrong about the arc, and just then Brent jumped up and ran forward. "Hey," he said. "Hey, it's not supposed to do that. It's my marsh—" But he never finished the word because the flaming ball landed on his eye.

By the time Anne got to him the flame was out but the hot sugar still stuck to his eyelid. He was screaming and Jerry was running over, and somebody from the next campsite came with an ice pack and somebody else was telling her where the nearest hospital was.

The drive to the Emergency was terrible. Anne sat cradling Brent while Jerry drove through the beginnings of the storm. She would have told him to slow down, but she was too busy trying to comfort the boy.

"He'll be all right," Jerry said as they pulled into the hospital parking-lot. "Won't you, champ?"

Anne didn't say anything, just struggled out of the car, carrying Brent, who really was too big to be held like a baby. Jerry preceded her through the door, flagging down a nurse, attempting to take charge. But the doctor on call said no real damage had been done, ice water had been the right thing to put on the burn. Brent would indeed be okay: "Just be careful with the eye for a couple of days," he said.

"See?" Jerry said when they were back in the car and the rain was pouring down. "Didn't I say it would all right?"

"Shh," Anne said. "He's asleep."

But when they got back to the campground, she allowed Jerry to take Brent from her arms and rush him into the tent.

"Don't worry," Jerry said when she dashed to shelter too. "It's just a shower. This is a drought year remember." Because she was so relieved that things weren't worse, she almost smiled. And later in the tent with the thunder roaring in the distance, she listened almost happily to the wind rustle the cottonwoods and the rain dance on the tent. When Jerry reached out to pull her closer, she moved against him, too, turning her face to be kissed. He could do that to her. If you'd asked her, Anne would have called it love. She did not want to blame Jerry for what had happened.

In the morning Brent woke up first. He didn't cry exactly. He was sort of snuffling deep in his throat when she first heard him. Then she became aware that she was wet and cold and that something was dripping on her face.

"Christ," Jerry said. He turned over and bumped against her. "You forgot to tell me to put the rain fly on the tent."

She forgot! The next thing he would say was that the tent was her idea, and not one he'd scrounged from his aunt. She knew better than to argue with him when something needed to be done, though, so she concentrated her energies in getting them up and out of there, no matter what he had to say. In half an hour they were down the dirt road, across the bridge and back in town at the laundromat.

So that's why she was so glad to see their yellow ponchos head down toward the river. She watched from the dirty window at the front of the laundromat for a minute, and then she sat down in one of those rickety moulded plastic chairs you find in places like that. She got out her wallet and counted how much they had left: $56 to last until they got back to Montreal next Friday, not counting what they could put on the Esso credit card. But before she could work out how they were going to get by on that, there came a sort of vibration. It was a deep sound that Anne could feel with her feet as well as her ears, like the noise was coming through the ground too.

She stood up and turned around so she could look out the window again. Through the rain she could still see the yellow ponchos. They were down by the cottonwoods just south of the bridge. Nobody else was out. A lone car was coming up the street from the river, but aside from that it looked like the world had shut down on account of rain.

And then suddenly she saw the water surge and the cottonwoods collapse. And the yellow ponchos were gone. Disappeared. Nowhere to be seen.

Maybe you read about what happened next in the newspaper or saw the footage on TV. Most of the pictures were taken later. The water was red-brown like the countryside, except where the wind whipped the water up into white foam. Full of junk too: parts of buildings, trees, even a section of the bridge that somehow had air trapped under it.

But at that moment when the yellow ponchos disappeared Anne didn't have any idea what was happening. She was paralyzed. She felt like she was suffocating. She couldn't believe what she'd seen. No time to build levees, no time to get to high ground. Just that: a wave of water.

In a drought year.

She ran out of the laundromat, calling their names even though the wind slapped them back in her face By the time she had run halfway to the bridge, she was in water up to mid-calf.

She would have kept going then, but the man at the service station just before the bridge yelled for her to stop. For a second Anne hesitated. Then, however, that one lone car stopped and then the man got out and then he and the gas station man were hustling her into the service station office. The water was still rising.

Inside they tried to raise the RCMP on the telephone. Anne was screaming something about Jerry and Brent being swept away. The service station man looked over at her and told her to can it, that he wouldn't be able to hear anybody who answered. But no-one did. "Lord knows where everybody is," he said finally. "Probably up near Morrin where the dam started to go this morning."

Afterwards Anne remembered thinking that she had no idea where Morrin was, but she didn't like the idea of a dam breaking.

"Yeah, got to evacuate all the low-lying territory," the other man said. "Did you see how the water rose just now? Wouldn't be surprised if that was the crest from there. 'S not easy, trying to hold back a dam that's fixing to bust."

"Anybody got a boat around here?" he added.

There *had* been an upturned rowboat on a lawn quite a distance from the river; Anne had noticed it when they crossed the bridge because it seemed so out of place. But, she realized, it probably was right at the edge of the water now. She was out the back door and down the hill before the men put their hats on and started after her.

You probably saw the helicopter rescues on the news. There's one in particular that Anne likes: the helicopter keeping right up with the roof of a house which is floating

68

down the river. There's a woman on top. They've lowered a man in a bosun's chair, and he's trying to reach down and get her, and she's stretching with all her might, but it doesn't look like it's going to work. Then the roof jams into the branches of a tree that's submerged but still standing. That slows things down just enough for the man hanging from the helicopter to grab hold of the woman. Incredible stuff. You think any minute the helicopter is going to crash in the water and everybody will be washed down the river.

But that must have happened a couple of hours later, when the peak of the water from the dam had passed and the river was just swollen with all the rainwater. Maybe toward sunset even: it took a while to get the rescue crews in, after all.

By then, it didn't make much difference to Anne. She doesn't think she even saw what the river looked like while she was on it. What she remembered afterwards comes in flashes. Trying to get the rowboat turned over. Fishing the oars out from underneath. Climbing in and then suddenly having the water carry her away.

But then she more or less got control. She picked her way along, keeping out of the main current. Out in the middle part of the river something went floating by, riding high, then crashing low in the thick of the current. If you got hit by something like that you'd never wake up. Jerry was a strong swimmer but if you're knocked out there's not much you can do. And Brent couldn't swim at all. Fear as cold as the water enveloped her.

How far the water carried her, she couldn't tell, but after a while she realized that the boat was riding lower and lower in the water. The rain was filling it up, and she had nothing to bail with.

She almost panicked then. She saw the yellow ponchos again in her mind, she felt the river pulling at her then and there. She knew her only hope would be to find a place to bring the boat to shore. She began to wonder: What if I can't make it? What if the boat fills up and I have to swim for it?

You know all those stories about drowning men having their lives flash in front of them? Not true. Instead you think about what matters to you. You concentrate on that, you think about the people you love and you want to cry over the things that you should have done and the other things you shouldn't have done. Remorse, regret. Guilt.

But Anne didn't pray that Jerry and Brent would be saved. Anne prayed that this terrible thing happening to them wasn't her fault.

Jesus, how selfish that sounds. Afterwards she was ashamed of it, but it's true. She has to face that. She had to face that, sitting by Brent's bed, waiting for him to wake up. Listening to Jerry rant and rave about what should be done to improve rescue work. Lying in bed, trying to sleep while Jerry talked on the phone to the lawyers, talking about the court case against the dam builders.

(There were five people killed that afternoon, and 36 houses washed away. Gone in half an hour, lifetimes of work and love and you name it. Just disappeared, the way the yellow ponchos disappeared by the cottonwoods.) So there she was, swirling along with the rushing water, praying and crying and trying to get the rowboat over to the edge of the river before it sank. All the wide spots in the river valley were filled with water so the shores were the hills. She aimed for an eddy she saw upstream from a canyon which was spilling a torrent into the river.

And then Anne saw a yellow poncho about three feet above the water line. A small yellow poncho. No sign of Jerry.

She yelled out: "Brent." Nothing moved, there was no indication he heard, but just the sight of the poncho was enough to keep her from giving up. The rowboat drifted toward a clump of branches and roots caught up on the remains of a tree. She reached out to grab them, and then she started to pull the boat through the water from branch to branch, hoping that she'd make it close enough to shore so she could jump out and pull the boat onto the land.

Before she made it to the shore, though, she heard a shout and looked up. There was Jerry standing near the top of the hill, waving at her.

God, she was glad to see him! She didn't even wonder why he was up there, and not down at the river's edge, trying to do something to help Brent. He ran down and helped her bring the rowboat up and then they sort of rocked back and forth in each other's arms. "I'm sorry," Anne said, over and over. "I'm sorry I was angry."

He didn't say anything at all. For once he cried and his words, of which ordinarily he had so many, seemed to melt with the rain and the tears.

They weren't airlifted out until the next morning, but the night wasn't too bad even though Brent was still semiconscious. Before sunset, a plane spotted them, and dropped a box with food and space blankets and water purification tablets. The helicopters were too busy saving the people stranded on rooftops and in trees to worry about them right away. And there was no way of letting them know that Brent was injured.

So you see, it wasn't as dramatic as a helicopter rescue, particularly that one Anne's mother taped. The man hanging from the helicopter, the woman on the roof. He, trying to reach down and get her, and she, stretching with all her might. And then everything slowing down as the roof jammed into the branches. It wasn't like any of that.

There wasn't anything really all that wrong with Brent either, in the end. The doctor who treated him at the rescue station (the same one who'd been on call at the hospital when they went in with his burnt eye) said it was lucky that the water was so cold. Slows the body down, he said. That's why Brent could survive not breathing for so long, and why when he came out of the coma there was so little damage done.

It was scary, Brent says now that he can remember again. One second they were wading along at the edge of the river, splashing away. Yes, they were splashing. Jerry had told him that he didn't have to worry about getting his shoes wet because they were already wet. That there wasn't anything to worry about because the cottonwoods' feet were wet already too, Brent says Jerry said.

And then he doesn't remember any more, not the wave of water, nor the wave of fear which must have engulfed him too. Protective amnesia, the social worker says. Better for him that way, probably.

And if he wants to watch CNN now, let him, she says. This flood is not his flood, but he's got to work it through himself.

Jerry's right arm was broken and the ligaments in his right shoulder were torn. That probably happened when he was trying to wedge Brent up into the fork of the tree branches, he says. That's what saved them: hanging onto one of the trees that was washed away with them. The tree Anne got hung up on as she tried to land the boat. Coincidence. A bit of luck they ended up at the same place.

Jerry says he doesn't believe in luck. If Brent is alive it's because he, Jerry, knew artificial respiration, because he dragged Brent out of the water and breathed into his mouth again and again until Brent spluttered back to life. No, luck has nothing to do with it, he says, and Anne has not asked him what he was doing at the top of the hill or where he was going.

But somebody is responsible for the dam failing, he says, somebody ought to pay. For a while he spent a lot of time on the phone, talking to many people—the families of people who were killed, the merchants in the town, the lawyers. He had time to do that, because his shoulder took a long time to heal. And he was out of work anyway, remember.

Anne's boss was pretty good about the time she lost. When her mother called to explain, he gave Anne four more days off with pay. The next week she had to take on her own account, but what can you expect?

By then Brent was out of the hospital, and Anne figured Jerry could look after him because Brent still was too shaky to go to the daycare centre. That was when they had the first fight. Jerry was home; he had no place else to go, nothing else to do. "But taking care of kids? Hey, that's woman's work," he said.

Those were his exact words. Of course, he'd said the same sort of thing before, the morning of the flood even. Anne had forgotten until then, but once again she saw him and Brent headed out the door. "Laundry is woman's work anyway, champ," he'd said. That's what made Anne so mad, that's the straw that broke the camel's back.

Yes, Anne likes to watch the videos of the newscasts. She likes to see the helicopter keeping right up with the roof of that house floating down the river. Anne likes to see the man in the sling hanging from the copter, trying to reach the woman on top. Anne likes to see her stretching, trying to make the connection, trying to be rescued. Anne likes to see things slow down. Just slow down. And then the man hanging from the helicopter grabs hold of the woman, and saves her. Tragedy averted.

Oh, damn. Life goes on. For a while Anne kept stretching too, she kept trying to make the connection, hoping that somebody would be there for her to rely on. But there was only Jerry. Laundry is woman's work, champ. Don't worry about getting your feet wet. Head over the hill and leave your son behind.

73

Oh shit, Anne knows why he did it, why he does it. Life isn't easy for him either. But when she realized that nobody was going to rescue her, she decided she had to rescue herself.

It's midnight, and Anne goes in and turns off the television without saying anything to Brent. He's curled up on the couch, sucking his thumb, not quite asleep. He's too big to suck his thumb, but the social worker says not to bug him about it. The last image before the picture fades is water flowing through a break in a levee somewhere.

He doesn't resist when Anne pulls him up and starts him walking toward his bedroom. He doesn't even say anything until he's in bed and Anne bends over to give him a kiss goodnight.

"Do you think Dad is watching CNN, Mom?" he asks, wrapping his arms around her neck tight.

"Sure," Anne says, reaching behind her head to loosen his hands so she can break free. "Sure thing, champ."

Manifest Destiny

The car doors were locked. Even from where she stood at the edge of the embankment, Lucy could see that the buttons were pushed down. Her mother would be all right. She had the radio on, there was no-one around besides the park maintenance crew cleaning the bathrooms. It wasn't too hot, it wasn't too cold.

Yes, her mother would be all right. She had even agreed she would be. "Go take your walk," she'd said. "Don't worry about me."

Nevertheless Lucy stifled the impulse to check again. Bad conscience acting up. But for Lord's sake, she ought to take advantage of this. When was the last time she'd taken a walk by herself?

She turned to look for a path that led to the beach. Too long, was the answer. Two weeks at least.

That was when she caught sight of the seal, swimming north. At least she thought it was a seal: a dark sleek form just beyond the breakers, barely visible through the morning fog, still hanging over the water.

She found herself smiling for the first time in a while. The last time she and Gordon and the kids had been down to San Diego, they'd watched a harbour seal basking on the deck of a small sailboat. A thief who took bait off fishermen's lines, who wouldn't be chased away, who appropriated any small boat it pleased, according to the man who ran the hotdog concession. But the kids had wanted to come back and see it every afternoon.

They still talked about it, four years later. They'd wanted to come too, this time, but of course it was out of the question. They were in school and Lucy had too much work to do, moving her mother. The move into the residence was done now, Lucy would be going back to Montreal in a few

75

days, she would see them all. She shouldn't be resentful that her mother wanted to come with her this Sunday morning, too, when she'd promised herself one last walk on the beach.

But this beach couldn't be a good place for seals, though, Lucy realized as she watched the animal rise and fall in the surf. The State Park was the most extreme south-western point in the Continental United States. Ocean currents here swept sewage up from Tijuana, and from the embankment, Lucy could see that the beach was littered with black splotches of oil from offshore drilling. She also saw white plastic bottles, small plastic tampon applicators, long strings of kelp, a pile of feathers that probably was a dead bird.

Lucy shivered and not just from the fog remaining in the air. She pulled her sweater tighter around her shoulders, and held her car keys so they projected through her fingers like the spikes on brass knuckles. She was sure there was no reason to be afraid, this was a well-patrolled State Park, there was absolutely no other car around, nobody would walk two miles from the road in Southern California even to get a beach. Maybe even especially to get to a beach, since there were so many of them.

Which of course brought up the question why she had chosen this beach to come to.

Partly to annoy her mother, she had to admit, because she had really wanted to go to the beach by herself. But her mother had assumed she was going too, and Lucy had given in without arguing. Certainly, if her mother's aim had been to irritate, she'd succeeded. Moreover, as soon as the woman had seen the freeway signs for the south county towns, she'd started in again about how Ava had deserted her, how you couldn't trust people like that, how the country would be better off without any of them, how it was bad enough in towns but down here near the border....

76

Her parents had become such bigots in the ten years they'd lived in California. Was it catching? Was it something in the water? She didn't remember them being so awful about Mexicans and Blacks and....

But no, Lucy was not going to think about Ava or her mother right now. She started down the path that leads to the beach. The path was not a deserted one, obviously people used it a lot. Not only was it well worn but also it was littered with soft-drink cans and the bright scraps of corn-chip bags....

Lucy avoided looking at the litter and concentrated on the other sensations. The air smelled of licorice and rot. The first came from the foliage, the second from the river which the road into the park had followed, past barren strawberry fields, past places where water pooled in the riverbed. Some water must flow all year round.

That surprised her. One of the shocks when she came to visit her parents after they moved was the tap water. It was imported from Colorado over 200 miles and tasted of magnesium. She remembered gasping at the taste the first time. But she also remembered seeing the names of streams on the map: the Otay, San Diego, San Dieguito, Santa Margarita and San Luis Rey rivers. All those streams coming out of the dry hills, stream beds lined with greenery even in the summer. Ending at the bay, which here owed its existence to the sediments deposited by the streams and which formed a long barrier peninsula. She had a sudden vision of how inviting the land must have looked 200 years ago when Spaniards set up their missions, when the Indians hunted and gathered.

The Americans had tried to take Montreal about then. If they had, a lot would be different....

But it wasn't a time for historical or philosophical musings. Lucy pushed on. The plants muffled the boom of the surf, and when the sun broke momentarily through the fog, she felt the heat untempered by a breeze off the water. Suddenly, just when she wondered how long the path could go on, she found herself at the edge of a bulwark of rocks. Below lay a short stretch of beach. Beyond that: the breakers. Where a head still bobbed, half hidden by a swirl of fog. The seal?

No, no, not a seal, but someone body-surfing, she told herself. Somebody who couldn't resist the long expanse of sand, running northwards so beautifully. But even as she began to invent the idea of such a somebody, she thought of sewage in the water. She would have gagged, but the rustle in the reeds stopped her. She froze. She searched with her eyes, suddenly too afraid to move.

There was a man watching her. There, over there, half hidden in the reeds. His hair was black, and so was his skin except around his eyes, where his real colour showed through, The pupils were dark too, but the whites glowed. He wasn't as tall as she was, and he was hunched over as if trying to make himself smaller. He was barefoot and wearing only a black T-shirt and jeans. His arms had been greased like his face: camouflage, she thought. What you did when you didn't want to be seen at night.

It was daylight, though.

Someone shouted, louder than the roar of the breakers. She looked toward the noise, south, toward. One of the maintenance crew was waving his arms, calling something she couldn't understand.

She tried to see what or who he was calling to, but she heard another rustle in the grass, saw the glint of the knife as it was drawn. The blackened face split in the middle as the man stepped toward her, grimacing.

She wanted to scream, but she couldn't. All she could think of was what her mother would say about her being killed on a beach near the border. Her mother would find it either embarrassing or ridiculous, would blame her for doing something that reflected badly on the family, or on some standard of behaviour that no-one had been able to define in 30 years.

Poor old woman, Gordon said after Ava left and Lucy's mother had telephoned in a panic. Ava had come to clean and cook only three days a week, but without her help the old woman was locked inside her arthritis and her memories. Poor Ava, too, he added; too bad she never got her immigration status fixed. (What an irony in that! Lucy's parents had no such problem when her father decided that California was where he wanted to retire eventually: a transfer by his company, a few forms filled out and her parents were legal.) And, Gordon added, your mother needs your help, go and get her settled in some place decent. I'll hold down the fort.

Lucy had already decided she wouldn't tell him about everything her mother said: how she called his father an old drunk (true enough but never said aloud), how she accused him, Gordon, of instability because he'd changed jobs a half-dozen times, how she railed against Ava for deserting her, even though it seemed pretty clear Ava had only left because Immigration was after her and her husband.

Lucy wasn't going to say anything about the underwear either. She had found mounds of it when she began to pack her mother's things. Three dresser drawers were filled with pants and slips and camisoles which her father had given her mother over the years, some of it still wrapped in tissue paper. Beautiful stuff but there was no point in keeping it, Lucy decided. None of it would fit because her mother was a shadow of what she'd been. Besides she doubted if her mother even realized it was there: Ava had done the laundry for the last three years, Ava put the everyday things in the one drawer that Lucy's mother could reach without getting out of bed.

So Lucy wrapped it all up with sweaters and old blouses

79

and what remained of her father's clothes and gave them to Ava's church for its next rummage sale. Ava was gone, nobody admitted knowing where she and her husband were hiding, but Lucy knew of no better place to get rid of the stuff.

The night before the move, however, Lucy heard a noise well after midnight. When she got to the doorway of her mother's bedroom, she saw her standing, crying, holding on to the edge of the dresser as if she would fall otherwise. "My things," she said, "my pretty things." She looked up as Lucy entered. "That slut took my pretty things."

"What slut? What things?" Lucy said. She knew, though, but she couldn't bring herself to explain just yet.

"Ava, the Mexican slut," her mother said. "She ran away, she deserted me. And she took my things."

It was pathetic. Even after Lucy explained what she'd done, her mother didn't understand. But then maybe being old was pathetic. This was not the time to reflect on the pathos of age, however. She had the man in front of her now. And his knife.

She took a deep breath. "You don't want to hurt me," she said. She took a step backward, trying to decide which way to run. Back to the parking-lot was sure safety but she would have to go through the weeds again. As long as the workman was up there, looking at the ocean, she'd be better off going toward the water where she'd be seen.

The man in front of her said nothing, and she realized that probably he didn't know much English. An illegal, a wetback: what else could he be? Same thing for the seal, the supposed-surfer out there in the water, she realized suddenly. Not a seal at all, another one trying to slip across the imaginary line out there, the border between the two countries. Greased up like Channel swimmers, they must have started down the coast, and swum north.

Lucy stood up straighter. She reached out her hand to the

man. "Give it to me," she said. She saw she probably could not win a fight with him because, although he was thin and obviously exhausted, he was desperate, and she wasn't. Nevertheless, she kept her hand held out and repeated; "You don't want to hurt me. Give it to me."

On the little bluff, the man from the park crew was screaming something. One of the other crew members was hurrying toward the edge too. She looked toward them, her concentration disturbed. The man in front of her shifted his weight, as he saw her distraction. "No," she said firmly as soon as she perceived his movement. "Don't do it."

The man's eyes held hers. Dark brown eyes with flecks of green in the irises. Tired eyes. She sensed just how much he resented her clean clothes, her well-fed aspect, her English, her presumption that he should give her something, simply because she asked.

The workmen had begun to jump from the low bluff down the beach, however, and the man looked over at them. This time she moved in the moment of distraction. She stepped forward on her left foot and brought her right knee up hard into his groin. He bent over, still holding the knife, but she turned and ran toward the beach.

The sand was soft, and she stumbled. She gasped for breath, and willed her legs to thrash forward because she was sure the man was behind her, ready to attack her. It was not until she reached the hard, wet sand where it was easier going, not until she was nearly even with the park workmen, that she realized the man was not likely to move out of his shelter. Especially not if he could see what was happening at the water's edge.

There the black thing she had thought was a seal washed back and forth where the waves, having broken their backs on the sandy bottom, beat raggedly on the shore. The taller of the two workmen was sitting down on the sand, taking off his boots, and rolling up his trousers. The other man was yelling something at him.

But he had been swimming, she told herself. The thing I saw was moving northward, was alive. Unless she had seen it just in its last minutes of exhaustion, just before it gave itself up to the currents and the waves, just yards away from its destination. Now it floated face downwards, and nothing moved except when rocked by the rising and falling water.

The tall workman waded out and pulled the body from the water. He and his partner stood for a moment, looking at it. The body looked short and dark-haired and greased black just like the other man in the reeds. It also looked quite dead; the taller worker nudged it slightly in the ribs with his foot.

Lucy knew, and she assumed the workers knew that when a person is drowning, you're supposed to put him on his back, pull out the tongue and breathe rhythmically into the mouth. But the men stood there, looking at the body, as if too ashamed or disgusted to touch this person, to put mouth to mouth, even though they had hurried to try to save him.

The illogic of that annoyed her. She started across the sand again. Before she realized it, she was kneeling next to the man, fishing his tongue out, pinching his nostrils shut and breathing into his mouth.

"Hey, cool it, lady," the taller workman began.

She looked up, and as she did the man on the ground choked, and vomited up a quantity of saltwater. Then, it was clear, he started breathing.

For a second she continued to kneel next to the man. Her hands were covered with grease and the front of her blouse was soaking wet. Poor guy. Like Ava's husband. Like Ava. No chance at the American dream.

She stood up, and suddenly she found herself shaking: her legs, her hands, her teeth. She was cold, she was exhausted, she realized that probably she was very lucky. "He

82

had a friend, hiding in the reeds over there," she nodded her head toward the bottom land. "He tried to jump me." The words were hard to say. She seemed to have lost control of part of her body: she couldn't stop shaking.

She had to wait while the Border Patrol looked for the man in the reeds (he was gone, as Lucy was sure he would be), and then they did the paperwork. There were questions about her immigration status too, but they were perfunctory. Nobody was going to suspect her of anything, she was explainable, she belonged, if not to the Greatest Country in the World, then to its best imitation, its northern neighbour.

She wondered what would happen to the other man. Paramedics took him away, but it wasn't clear if a hospital would admit him, or if he'd just be dumped across the border.

Twice during the wait Lucy went over to check on her mother, standing where the old woman wouldn't be able to see her. Her mother sat staring out at the stretch of sea and sky directly in front of her, her head no higher above the door frame than that of a child. Safe behind the locked doors.

Two brown pelicans patrolled the waves. The tide began to turn and after a while Lucy realized the beach was growing wider and dirtier as the receding water left behind more garbage on the sand. Then, a half-hour later, the officers were through and she could go.

"Where have you been?" her mother said when she unlocked the door. "I was dying in here of the heat. I hope you got enough exercise to last a while, because I don't intend to wait again."

Lucy nodded. "Of course," she said, not trusting herself to say anything more. It was only when she was behind the wheel with the key in the ignition that she looked over at her mother.

The woman was crying silently. Then she felt Lucy's eyes on her and she turned abruptly away. "Don't look," she said. "Don't remember me this way. I wasn't always like this."

They took I-5 up the coast on the way back, then cut over at Palomar Road. The residence was out in what still was almost country. Even on Sunday there were men in the fields, planting gladiolas, potting poinsettias, and, in one place wearing white contamination suits, goggles and hoods, spraying tomatoes.

The trip took longer than Lucy expected; the traffic coming back from the beaches was heavy. The road passed El Camino Real, passed the sign for the San Luis Rey Mission, passed a group of men waiting for the bus to take them home from the fields. Small, dark men, of course.

The afternoon smog had settled in, but Lucy still could see how the upland rolled off north and south, cut by the streams she'd seen on the map running down from the mountains to the sea: San Dieguito, Santa Margarita and San Luis Rey rivers, San Marcos creek, Agua Hedionda. All names, she noted, left by the Spaniards, who must have travelled the uplands when they went from one mission, one estancia to another. Long, long ago. At a time when Lucy's part of the world had been settled for 150 years, when the Indians, or Native people, or First Nations there had long been decimated by smallpox, with those who survived pushed into settlements quaintly called "reserves."

And the point is? she asked herself. More than names are left of that first wave of Europeans, French is the official language of Quebec. That, perhaps, is marginally better, because the power—some of it—is shared.

But people seal themselves in containers to try to enter Canada. They swim ashore when freighters dump them into the sea off Vancouver Island. There are so many in the world who have so little, and so few who have so much.

84

And those who have? Well, if they're smart they know 1) just how lucky they are, and 2) if there's any justice, a time may come when the tables are turned.

In the evening Lucy took her mother down to have dinner in the dining-room. Her mother walked slowly, but she was out of breath before they reached the door to the dining-room. She stopped, although not only (Lucy knew) because her old body needed to. She looked around the room: at the polished oak plank floor, the white stucco walls, the dark beams spanning the space end to end. At the potted plants in the corners, the yellow chrysanthemums on the tables, the white napkins, the 35 women and the three men waiting to be served their dinner. At the white hair and walkers, the stooped shoulders and shaking hands. And at the small dark women who would serve them.

Then Lucy's mother straightened up and started into the room as if she owned it. The waitress for her table smiled. Lucy smiled back. As if it would make a difference.

What Lil Remembers

Lil remembers this:

If she left the house at 7:15 she could make it to the hospital by 8 AM. The shift would have changed then, and if all had gone well, she could feed Jeffrey and bathe him and sit by his crib out of the nurses' way.

This, of course, meant taking the bus at the beginning of the rush hour, after taking Celia to the neighbour whose daughter would take her to the day-care centre on her way to school. The seats on the 80 bus were nearly always full no matter what the time but at least she got her own pole to cling to at that hour. She didn't have to concentrate on keeping her balance as the bus lurched its way down the street. She could worry about Jeffrey. George was away, and she was so tired that she had to scrape up little pieces of energy to get enough to worry properly about the baby.

On the second day of this routine, she remembers trying to avoid the guy whose boy was in the day-care with Celia. But it's hard to avoid acknowledging someone you know when you're standing hip-by-bum. She gave him only a tightlipped smile that first morning, and the second one she hurried to the back of the bus when she saw him get on a stop after she did. She didn't want anything to get in the way of her worrying. Worrying was the only thing she could do.

That afternoon, though, when she'd left Jeffrey and was on her way to pick up Celia she found, wonder of wonders, an empty seat halfway to the back of the bus. She sat down. She had no idea he was next to her. She told herself very clearly afterwards that seeing him surprised her.

Lil does not remember, usually, why she was so particularly tired that day, why she wanted to sit down so badly. It had to do with the child in the crib next to Jeffrey, though.

Jeffrey was out of intensive care, they'd decided that whatever had caused the convulsions was not related to an infectious disease. She should have been relieved.

Lil never remembers exactly what she said to the guy, or what he said to her. She knows that they walked along together from the bus stop to the day-care, though, and that he asked Celia if she'd like to have dinner at the souvlaki place with him and his son. "You go home and take a nap. I'll bring her by in an hour," he said to Lil so she suspects she must have told him about Jeffrey and the way his little body shuddered and twitched and burned with fever.

Did Celia want to go? Lil remembers that she did not. She clung to Lil, but Lil insisted. "You'll have a good time," she said. "You'll have a better supper than you'll get at home." She unwrapped Celia's hands which were tightly clutching Lil's coat. This wasn't what she and George had decided should be done, the way they'd both agreed that they needed to keep things as normal as possible for the little girl. But Lil didn't care at that point. She needed to sleep. She needed to make sense of what was wrong about the room that Jeffrey was in now.

She stood up. She picked Celia up. She handed her into the waiting arms of the guy, the boy's father. "Thank you," she said. She began to fish in her purse for money. "Here's a ten. Will that be enough?"

He may or may not have taken the bill. Certainly he took Celia with him. He took her with his son, and he made some kind of joke that the boy laughed at and at which Celia even smiled a little.

I must not feel guilty about this, Lil told herself, Lil remembers telling herself. I cannot help myself.

They say that about half the marriages that come up against the serious illness or disability of a child don't survive. Lil couldn't remember where she'd read that but she could believe it. Any little suspicion, any tiny doubt becomes as welcoming as a crack in the pavement is to an urban weed.

There was no question that what George was doing was admirable, that she supported it with all her heart. His dedication was one of the things that attracted her, she thought that he might be able to make a difference. He'd finished medical school just about the time they met, and she'd encouraged him to apply for the jobs with the aid groups. And for his second tour, she had been able to go along. The disaster was the aftermath of a hurricane in Central America this time, and an agency could use her because she knew Spanish. They had her finding supplies in the region, talking by radiophone to government ministries, going on talk shows back home by long distance. When the temporary infrastructure—pumps and waterlines, generators and electric connections for part of the refugee camp—was in place and her assignment was over, the head of the section told her he'd never worked with anybody more efficient. "Come back," he'd said. "I can always use people like you."

But at the end of their two months back in Canada, she'd discovered she was pregnant. Since then she'd stayed home, although she'd been scrupulous about encouraging George to take what assignments seemed most pressing.

Which is not to say that she wasn't pleased when he was able to arrange to be home for nearly six months after Celia was born, and for two months before and two months after Jeffrey's birth. "I wouldn't have missed this for the world," he told people.

And to give him credit, he offered to come back when she finally was able to locate him that awful day that Jeffrey started his convulsions. "I could be there day after tomorrow, I'm sure, sweetie," he said, the line crackling between them. This time he was doing a rotation in a refugee camp behind the lines of an African bush war so unstrategic that they hadn't seen a television crew in more than a year.

"No, no," she'd said. "Stay there. Everybody says he's going to be all right even though they want to keep him a couple of more days for observation." To her surprised disappointment he'd taken her words at face value and said he'd contact her at the same time the next day, just to make sure that everything was going all right.

But he didn't. There was a message relayed from the agency's headquarters that he'd been sent over to help with an outbreak of cholera a thousand miles away. "He said to tell you that he'll call as soon as he can," the agency person said. "And if you have any news, we can probably get it to him within a few hours, one way or the other."

Which left her with nothing to do but talk to her boss about taking at least another week off. Her mother had offered to come and help, and so had George's mother. But the last thing she wanted was to have to cope with a grandmother on the premises. Better to be exhausted than to be furious at advice you couldn't ignore.

Nevertheless she felt the doubts and the annoyance settle into the cracks in whatever it was that bound her to George. She would have to be on her guard.

Lil remembers the door bell ringing and the way she had to fight to swim up into consciousness. The guy, his son and Celia were at the door when she finally got there, and Celia was dancing from one foot to another, a box from the restaurant held carefully in her hands.

"We brought you supper, Momma," she said. "We wanted to make sure you had something good to eat too." Celia bounced through the door, and the boy followed her. Greg (because that was the guy's name) hesitated a moment at the door, but in a second entered, taking Lil's small smile as an invitation.

Celia was in the kitchen, pulling a chair over to the

counter so she could take a plate from the dishdrainer, handing it to the boy. "Put that on the table, and then we'll get the milk out of the refrigerator..." she was saying.

"Nice kid you've got," Greg said as he stood watching what the children were doing. "She said you were very tired and we should bring you something too."

"Thanks," Lil said. And then, to her surprise, she turned to him and began to cry.

The child in the bed next to Jeffrey's didn't look much like a child. She (the tag at the end of the bed said that her name was Pauline Martin) had a head which at the top was the size of an ordinary child's. The face narrowed though, through a nose which was not much more than two holes to a mouth which was not finished off with a jaw. She had been born more than two years before, according to the tag, but her body was no bigger than that of a year old. Her arms and legs were sticks; her fingers, webbed. She couldn't sit up, couldn't even hold her head up, but the worst thing about her, Lil thought, was her silence.

No vocal chords, the nurses said. We're not even sure how much she hears. But it's clear that she can't talk, can't even cry. She won't live long, they added: it'll be a blessing when she goes. Then they whispered, when Lil asked, that this was what happened sometimes when you took drugs when you were pregnant. Not that the mother hadn't tried to do right by the child after she was born. She'd tried to take care of her, she'd kept her at home for months, but in the end the damage was more than a normal person could deal with, let alone someone with a substance abuse problem.

Lil couldn't look when a nurse fed the child, spooning cereal into her mouth, holding her gingerly while she drank from a bottle. Instead, Lil sat so her back was to that crib, so that all she could see was Jeffrey, who was going to recover, who was going to be normal, who was perfectly all right. Who had to be protected from the evil loose in the world.

Or maybe it wasn't quite like that. Maybe she'd noticed Greg before and every time they rode down on the bus together, she'd smiled at him and he smiled back. There's nothing wrong with smiling at somebody you know, after all. It's only neighbourly, only friendly and the world is such a sorry place that it can do with as much neighbourliness as you can offer.

So that day when she found the empty seat on the bus beside him, she was ready to tell him everything, and ready to take him up on the offer when he suggested they order pizza in at his place once they'd picked up Celia and his son at the day-care. Then when they'd eaten, the kids went into the boy's room where they started some elaborate game which had to do with princesses and knights and rescuing magic horses from monsters. That meant the grownups could sit in the living-room and drink wine, which they did.

Lil remembers that Greg told her about his work, which had to do with computerized animation, and his ex-wife, who was a lawyer, and the custody arrangement, which gave Greg the boy on alternate weeks. She remembers that she explained about what George did, and how proud she was of him, and the way he'd volunteered to drop everything and come back when Jeffrey became ill.

She remembers that Greg listened to her carefully, that he refilled her wine glass twice, and that he reached for her hand when her voice broke as she told him about waking up to find Jeffrey in convulsions.

She remembers that his eyes were very blue and that her body, which had been straining toward something that she could not identify, suddenly relaxed. She remembers that she did not want to pull her hand away, but that she did. She remembers that Celia did not want to go home, but that they did. She remembers....

Not all the children on D Ward had mothers who could spend the entire day with them. There were several who arrived very early in the morning before they went to work, and helped get their kids ready for the day. They might bring Egg McMuffins from the McDonald's across the street for the two of them to eat together. Or they might spend half an hour brushing a daughter's hair and then plaiting it in French braids attached with fat bows.

There were others who came in the evening, sometimes with a video to watch together in the lounge at the end of the hall, sometimes with a pile of paperwork to do while the child watched television.

There were couples who spelled each other, one taking the day shift, the other, the evening, so that nearly always there was someone the child loved nearby.

There was one mother who spent all her time there, sleeping on a mat on the floor and eating in the hospital cafeteria. Where she washed, Lil wasn't sure. Her hair was stringy but from the singular lack of style in her clothes, Lil suspected that was its usual state and not the result of sacrifice. It was only the fire in her eyes that gave her away. No matter how demurely she avoided looking at you, her glance, if you intercepted it, proclaimed that she could not allow this to happen to her child and therefore the rest of the world must bear the consequences if he grew worse.

Some of the children had no visitors at all. Of these, at least five were kids flown South from the Montagnais and Inuit country because the treatment they needed couldn't be provided closer to home. The nurses as a group looked out for them, which wasn't unpleasant to do because they were basically healthy, cute children. They would be going home soon, they were going to be all right.

But there also were Pauline and a couple of others like her. Taking up space. Waiting. Souls already in limbo, with bodies abandoned by their earthly families.

Lil wrote to George about them. She decided that she would write as much as she could, to tell him what she was thinking, because she couldn't talk to him. Of course, he wouldn't receive the letters until Jeffrey was back home, until she'd picked up the pieces, and was back to dropping him off at the babysitter on the mornings and taking Celia to day-care afterwards. But it kept him present while she tried to cope.

She didn't write him about the dinner they had with Greg and his son. She didn't write him about how she hated to see Pauline eat.

Lil remembers the doctor telling her about high temperature convulsions in young children. Babies and toddlers can spike a fever easily. That's a shock to their brains, hence the convulsion. But just as quickly the fever can subside and in 95-98% of the cases there is no problem afterwards.

To find out though, you have to watch the child for a while, which is why Jeffrey was still in the hospital even though they'd determined that he didn't have meningitis or some other horrible thing. "It probably was due to those vaccines he'd had: it's a perfectly ordinary reaction. He's almost sure to be good as new inside a week," the doctor said. "Don't worry. And you, you take care of yourself, too. You don't want to get exhausted, running back and forth."

So she tried to conserve her energy. She'd already begun to wean him when he got sick, she'd cut him back to two feeds a day, so that strain was somewhat reduced. So what she'd do is give him his morning feed sitting next to his crib, and then she'd play with him and be glad he wasn't at the stage where he shrank from strangers. If he were it would have been that much harder to leave him at night. But at six months he would smile at a nurse or aide if one picked him up. If someone amused him or gave him a bottle it was as if he figured: well, I'll take whatever I can get. Nevertheless she was glad that he seemed to hold out his best smiles for her, that he snuggled most comfortably into her arms. That someone loved her the best.

Toward the end of the afternoon on the fourth day, though, when she was trying to interest him in shaking some coloured rings, she became aware of a sound besides his chortles and shrieks. It was a sort of snuffling and it came from behind her, from the crib where Pauline sat in a baby seat, staring at nothing.

Lil turned and as she did, she knocked the rings against the side of Jeffrey's crib, which somehow opened the latch on the central ring so they fell apart into half a dozen separate plastic circles. Jeffrey was not pleased. He too was sitting in a baby seat, and the rings fell just beyond his reach. He squealed and stretched.

Lil handed two of them to him, but on a whim she turned and also dangled two in front of Pauline. The child could not take the rings, but it was clear that her eyes followed when Lil moved them.

Jeffrey roared: he wanted his rings. When she handed them to him, he stuck them in his mouth and chewed happily. "My lovely, normal little boy," she said to him. She dropped the rings in the other crib and stood up so she could lean over Jeffrey and nuzzle him. "My lovely, normal sweetheart."

There was no message from George when she got home, and she debated calling the agency to see if there was any news from him. No-one was likely to be still in the office at this hour, though, and Celia said she was starving, so they agreed that they'd make pancakes for supper with Celia flipping them over. Halfway through, when they'd cooked enough for both of them but still had lots of batter left, Celia said: "Let's call our friends up and have them over."

"Our friends?" Lil knew who Celia meant, but she didn't dare say. Celia was fishing in the pocket of her jeans already, though.

"Here's the phone number," she said, holding up a tiny piece of paper. "They gave it me, just in case."

So Greg and his son came over.

Physical attraction is hard to explain. Lil had never been able to say why George had caught her eye the first time she met him, but he had. Even before she learned what he did, she wanted to know him. And now she was up against the same sort of thing with Greg. He stood, leaning against her refrigerator while the kids ate pancakes, and drank a beer. He was listening to her tell about Pauline, but there was an unspoken conversation going on too.

"So I wonder, it must feel awful to have a child like that on your conscience," she said. "To think that something you did was responsible for imprisoning a soul in that dreadful body."

He took a pull on his beer. "Oh, the mother probably doesn't feel all that bad. I mean, you couldn't, could you? You'd have to rationalize it some way, blame it on fate or bad luck or whatever." He looked at her. "Besides, souls and bodies: who knows what the link is there."

Souls and bodies, souls and bodies. "I don't feel very well," she said to him, as she suddenly felt her legs buckle under her.

There is a conversation that Lil usually does not remember. It was between George and herself and it took place the evening before he left the last time. She had wanted to go out to dinner with him, but he wanted to eat with the kids. "When's the next time I'll be able to sit down with them?"

95

he asked. "I want to see my children."

She might have argued but what was the point? He had the habit of authority, and she had the habit of accommodation. This one evening was not going to be the time to change. The meal, however, was not what he expected, because Celia, too excited by half from the attention of her father, couldn't sit still. "I want to sit on your lap, Daddy." "Can you feed me, Daddy." "Do you want to see how fast I can eat that, Daddy."

Jeffrey, who still was tiny, nevertheless sensed the tension in the air, and screamed every time Lil tried to put him down.

"Nurse him, damn it," George said, as she tried to hold him while she put food for George and Celia on the table. "Can't you see that he's starving?"

"Just a second, just a second," she said. Everything was on the table except the milk. She reached over George to pour his glass, then turned to fill Celia's. As she did, the blanket Jeffrey was wrapped in trailed on the table, knocking over George's glass. He leaped to his feet to avoid the milk which spread over his plate, drowning the shrimp and snow peas she'd cooked for supper.

"Jesus, Lil, is this madhouse what you want me to remember?" he shouted.

She looked up from the spilled milk, which she was trying to wipe up. "What did you say?" she asked, although she'd heard very well.

"Is this what you want me to remember? Mess and screaming?"

She stood up and faced him. "Oh, shit," she said. "You don't care about us. You just want to go off and be a hero," she said.

"Hero? Is that what you think I'm doing? You ought to know better, you've been there in the field. It's dirty and discouraging and godawful. And, you, all you have to do is

96

enjoy life here, with your kids and your running water and the meat and vegetables that you can buy at the market where there's never any shortage. You're lucky, woman, you don't know how lucky you are."

The phone rang then: details about the departure the next day, and at that moment, Lil had been glad for the diversion of his wrath. Only later, when he came back from running a last-minute errand and crawled into bed next to her did she realize just how neatly he had already escaped. They made love, but she had to ask for it.

Lil forgot that, though.

When she collapsed, Greg carried her into the bedroom and sat next to her on the bed, once he'd laid her down. She was aware of what was happening: her head was turning but she still heard the kids playing at the other end of the apartment, she still knew that Celia needed a bath before she went to bed, she remembered that she had wanted to do a couple of loads of washing.

Nevertheless she made no attempt to sit up when she began to feel less fragile. She didn't pull her hand away this time when he reached over to take it. She even smiled at him when he looked questioningly at her.

"Yes," she said. "Please do," even though she was only vaguely aware what the question was.

He began to take off his shoes and socks, but then stopped: "Wait a second," he said before he went to the door to listen for the children. The television appeared to be on: time for "South Park"—usually forbidden, but she didn't care.

"We have half an hour probably," he said, as he came back to the bed after closing the door.

She nodded, and then began to pull off the sweater she was wearing.

The only light came from the streetlight shining in the window, which didn't reveal how her belly still was slack from carrying Jeffrey. But Greg didn't need light to touch her breasts, bigger and more beautiful than they ever were when she wasn't nursing. More sensitive too, more delightfully responsive to everything he did to them.

(She had forgotten this, too: that she had been ravenous for George when she'd been pregnant, that sex with him after Celia was born had been better than before.)

A half-hour: enough time, but not enough.

When the television program was over, Greg told Celia that her mother wasn't feeling well. The three of them—Greg, his boy and Celia—would do the dishes and then he and his son would leave so that Celia could get ready for bed by herself. "When you've got your pyjamas on and brushed your teeth, go in and give your Mom a kiss," Lil heard Greg say when they'd finished in the kitchen. "She'd like that."

Celia seemed not upset by the idea. "She likes kisses," she said, as she went with them to the front door.

"I bet she does," Lil heard Greg answer. Then he added, just before she heard the door click shut, "Tell her to give me a call if she needs any more help."

The next morning Lil refused to think about the night before. Instead she carefully concentrated on thinking about what Celia wanted and needed and then, when she got to the hospital, on Jeffrey. That became easier in mid-morning when the doctors on their rounds announced that Jeffrey could go home that afternoon provided the last blood test was clear, which everyone expected it to be. "The convulsions were just a reaction to his shots," the resident repeated.

When they'd passed on, Lil picked Jeffrey up and danced around with him. "My lovely normal little boy," she said.

"You're going home. We're going home."

And the baby, who knew something was up, chortled and sang along with her.

They had to wait for the test results, though, which made the morning long. Lil played patty-cake and peek-a-boo with him and tried to show him the pictures in a little book she'd found among the playthings in the toy cupboard near the nurses' station. Then she saw the coloured rings that he'd been playing with the day before. They had fallen on the floor in the end, and had been swept under the cabinet in the corner, so that you couldn't see them easily.

Getting down on her hands and knees, Lil rescued them, and then washed them in the sink with lots of hot water and soap, the way the woman who took care of toys showed her. Jeffrey seemed glad to see them, so she rigged a sort of mobile across the bars of his crib so they hung within reach and he could bat at them.

When she finished and was standing watching her baby's concentrated delight, she became aware of something else going on. At first she felt uncomfortably as if she were being spied on. But, no, there was no-one watching through the glass partitions, no medical or nursing students observing, no curious parent wondering what was going on.

But the feeling didn't go away. In fact, it began to grow to a suspicion that somehow someone besides Greg and herself knew what had transpired between them. Nonsense, of course: the kids had watched the forbidden program until Greg went down to recruit them for the dishes. No-one could have seen in the window. No-one could know. What had happened was a guilty secret, but a secret it would remain. Something she would forget in a few weeks time, something she could not allow herself to remember. Particularly not now when everything was going to be all right.

Then behind the happy noises that Jeffrey was making she heard the snuffling she'd heard before. She steeled herself to turn and look at Pauline, who this morning had been propped up so she lay on her side.

The child caught her eyes, and held them with an expression that mixed shame and sorrow and great pain.

Lil stared back into her eyes, mesmerized by what she saw. No, the child who suffered so terribly from adult sins and transgressions, could know nothing about Lil's secrets. But she did know something else.

"You heard us talking about going home, didn't you?" Lil said, leaning over the crib. "You understand that much, don't you?"

There was no answer of course. The child, remember, had no vocal chords. But a stream of tears began to flow out of her right eye, running down her face, coursing into her misshapen nostrils.

Lil was repulsed, she was ready to turn away. However, as the child began to choke on her own tears, Lil found herself leaning over the bar of the crib, and picking her up. "Poor thing," Lil said. "Poor, poor thing. I'm sorry, I'm so very sorry."

She held her and rocked her, until the nurse came with lunch and the news that Jeffrey's last test was good.

"Can someone come and pick you up?" the nurse asked. "If not, we'll see that there's a cab downstairs when you're ready to go."

For just a second, Lil allowed her mind to light on Greg's name. But, no, she knew better. "We'll take a cab," she said, putting Pauline back in her crib, putting all that behind her.

Afterwards she and Jeffrey left the hospital to improvise the rest of their lives. In this they were joined immediately by Celia and eventually by George, who, it should be added, had memories quite different from Lil's.

Evening Star, Winter Nights

Looking good and love are the two most important things, so Lani turns up the volume on the smile, even though she's shivering. It's very cold out of the sun and her jacket just covers her butt, but she knows she looks good. She wanted to look good for Alex. She always wants to look good for Alex, because she loves him.

Alex, however, notices neither the smile nor the shiver "Where is it?" he says.

She reaches in her pocket and pulls out her passport, clean and unused. It dates back to the trip that her father talked about but which never materialized, back to the time when he still lived at home, when her mother was only beginning to get fat. "You promise I'll get it back...."

"Sure, sure," Alex says, reaching for the document.

She had expected that he would do something nice at that point: give her a hug, kiss her on the cheek. After all, she is foxing class for him, she has just saved his skin. But he doesn't. He turns and goes.

The pool-hall is two streets over and the sidewalk is icy in places, so Lani grabs at Alex's sleeve when they get to the corner. "Wait up," she says.

He pulls his arm away and says nothing, but he waits. His face looks pale, she sees out of the corner of her eye. He's scared, she thinks. Then he pulls the passport from his pocket and waves it. "This is what he wants now, but it isn't going to be enough, you know."

"Not enough," she says. His eyes are light blue with circles under them which are a darker blue. He needs a shave: she hasn't noticed that ever before. She shivers again.

The boys began coming after Lani when she was eleven or twelve. Her mother Rosie wasn't surprised: same thing happened with her when she was that age. The big guys just came sniffing around, it was sort of a compliment, nothing to get upset about. Rosie had liked the attention: it felt good.

And when Lani was that age, she needed attention too, Rosie figured. Dennis moved to California when she was eleven, when Mitchell was sixteen and Sean was fifteen. None of them liked Dennis moving, Mitchell wanted to go with him even, but you can imagine what Dennis' reaction was. He hadn't had much to do with the kids for the last couple of years, ever since he and Rosie split up, and he wanted even less to do with them when he was going to start a New Life.

That was a winter from hell for Rosie. Mitchell got picked up for shoplifting and Sean would disappear for two or three days at a time. Oh, he'd call about eleven o'clock and say that he was okay, but he wouldn't say where he was going to spend the night. He only told Rosie last summer that he'd go to the Emergency-room at one of the hospitals and sit around from midnight to 6 AM. Only once did anybody ask who he was waiting for, and then he made up a story about his girlfriend's baby. He was all right, and he didn't get into any real trouble, but you can imagine how Rosie worried.

So you can see what a blessing Lani was at that point. She got up in the morning, and she washed her hair and headed off to school without any big drama. Most nights she was there when Rosie came home from work, too, sitting at the kitchen table doing her homework. Rosie would think, thank God for her. At least I've got my little star, my heavenly flower. (That's what Leilani, which is her full name, means, you know. There's always been this special link between her and Rosie since before she was born, since that morning Rosie woke up and saw this star shining through the window directly down on them.)

But anyway, she was a good girl, and Rosie certainly wasn't thinking about her and boys or her and other kinds of trouble when the phone rang at work. Not that Rosie heard it, because there she was, with a steady stream of people coming in and out of the store, and Rosie punching away at the cash register, trying to be polite. But then the manager came out of the office and told her that the principal had called.

An accident! That's what Rosie thought, of course. The manager—she's got kids too, she's a good sort—said not to worry, to go ahead, leave right away. She even lent Rosie ten bucks for the cab, because it was the end of the month and Rosie was pretty near broke.

It only takes about five minutes by car to get to the school, so she just sat on the edge of the seat, trying to hold herself together, telling herself it couldn't be too bad or else they'd have said to go straight to the hospital. She was shivering, she could see Lani stretched out in the schoolyard, knocked out from hitting her head when she fell, or unconscious because a science experiment went wrong, or running a massive fever picked up from some poor, maltreated kid. When Rosie saw a police car in front of the school and another one coming the other way as they pulled up, she thought: where's the ambulance? Has it already left?

The three steps down into Champ's are ice-coated, and Lani clutches at Alex's arm. Making an entrance on your ass would be no way to start things right. Alex doesn't seem to notice that she grabs at him. All his muscles are tense and he walks through the door without even nodding to the two guys leaning against the wall, even though Lani knows he knows them.

Bingo's the one to see, and Bingo is over in the corner, standing at the bar, leaning on in it, looking calm and unhurried. Alex sees him immediately, Lani knows, but he doesn't say anything until he's standing in front of Bingo. "Here it is," he says, holding out the passport.

Bingo takes it, but otherwise ignores Alex. Instead he smiles at Lani, and strokes her arm the way you'd pet a cat. "Such a very pretty girl," he says. "We're always glad to find pretty girls like you."

Lani looks away from Bingo. His eyes glitter. You cannot find warmth in eyes that glitter.

"No," Alex says. "You promised. The passport would be enough."

"For now," Bingo says. He turns his gaze from Lani to the boy. "There is always another time...."

"I want a letter," Alex says. "Or a receipt or something. Proof that I paid."

"Ah, but you must understand, I don't keep any written records." Bingo's hand is on the little booklet, his smile is broader than ever. "Imagine what would happen if written things fell into the wrong hands. Imagine the embarrassment to you, to her, to your families. Besides," Bingo says, "I am a man of honour. You must trust me at my word." And he laughs.

Lani watches Alex's face buckle under the onslaught of worry and uncertainty. She is so wrapped up in that she does not hear the voices raised at the pool table near the door. She does not even hear the approach of the sirens.

You have to ring a bell to get into the school. The secretary can see you from her office, and she's supposed to press a button to unlock the door if she thinks you look like you have legitimate business. But the door was open when Rosie went up the steps, and a policewoman stood beside it. She nodded to her as she came in: "The principal's office is to your right," she said.

Rosie knew that already: Lani was her third kid to go to

the school after all. But she'd never been greeted by a cop.

The halls were empty because it was during class time, and for just a second Rosie felt guilty but also joyful, the way she remembered feeling the times she cut classes. God, she thought, 25 years and I still haven't got over school.

The door to the principal's office was open and Rosie was just about to reach in so she could give a little polite knock on it when the cops who'd been arriving just as she did surged into the hall.

"Down there," she heard the policewoman at the door say, and then two big guys in uniform pushed past her. "They're waiting for you."

Lani is aware of the cops' arrival only when the door swings open and the cold air sweeps in. She looks over to see one cop, two cops, three cops coming down the couple of steps from street level, while the two who arrived first stand at the door with their pistols drawn. "Freeze," they both shout.

She freezes, she would have anyway. She doesn't move until a policeman comes over and pushes Alex to the wall. Then she realizes, as he lets go of her hand, that her fingers have no more feeling.

A couple of years ago, the time when Rosie was so concerned about Sean, there were two or three shooting galleries on Park Avenue. How did she know? The boys never said anything, and to be honest she didn't want to know if they knew about them, not first-hand at least. But at the big pharmacy they put up a sign saying that they didn't sell needles without a prescription, that the nearest needle exchange was downtown. The sign had a telephone number too, and once when Rosie went in to get her high-blood-pressure medicine she saw this skinny little woman writing it down. Or trying to, because she was jerking around like her body was trying to get away from her. Pathetic.

The one thing Rosie gave Dennis credit for was the fact that he never was involved in anything like that. He nearly quit a job once because the boss wanted him to be, what do you call it, a mule? One of those guys who brings in drugs illegally. Dennis and Rosie and the kids were supposed to go down to one of the islands and they'd give Dennis some toys to switch with the kids' things. Nobody'd check them, they looked too honest. But Dennis said no as soon as he got the details, although he didn't tell Rosie for months later. All she knew was that suddenly this trip they'd been hoping for wasn't going to happen. Now she thought it was one of the better things he'd done.

Not that he ever was against having a good time. Rosie's family lived on the third floor of a triplex and her room was the one in the back. For one whole year every Friday night Dennis would come up the outside stairway, which was enclosed in a shed. The door from it to the balcony was supposed to be always locked, but Rosie'd go out and open it. About midnight there he'd be, tapping on the window. They had some sweet nights then. But the difference is: Rosie was eighteen and he was twenty-one.

Lani is only fourteen.

And she had always been a good girl, a special girl. Rosie never worried about her and boys and drugs at all. Up until they let Rosie see her she was sure the girl had been in an accident.

The dog doesn't look particularly frightening. A German Shepherd, but his tongue's lolling out and his eyes look more friendly than searching. Lani lets him sniff her up and down, she considers putting out her fingers for him to lick. The policeman holding the leash is more scary. What's worse, she can't see what's happening to Alex, she'll die if anything bad happens to him.

When her turn comes, the officer asking the questions looks at her carefully before he tells her to take off her coat, her boots, to put her backpack on the table in front of her. She knows what they're going to do, she knows what they're looking for, and she's glad that she has nothing on her.

Somebody behind her is whimpering, she hopes it isn't Alex. "What're you doing out of school?" the cop asks. "They don't let you out until 3:30." A statement, not a question.

She decides to attempt a grin; it helps so much of the time. "Sometimes they do."

"Today is not one of them," he says, running his hand inside the pockets in her backpack. "Where's your ID?" he asks. "What's your excuse for being here at all?"

Alex is sitting on the window ledge at the front now. He's handcuffed, she sees. So are all of the guys who'd been playing pool.

Where's Bingo? Where's Bingo? She knows that the real reason the cops are here has to do with Bingo, not her, and it would be terribly unfair if he got away again. She'd heard about the time two of his pretty girls were picked up on Saint Denis street near the Beaubien Metro station and he just disappeared down the stairs toward the trains. Bastard! Alex had told her that, when he'd been explaining why he had to have the passport. He had tears in his eyes, he said he never wanted her to be a situation like that.

The cop, however, has come at last upon her wallet with her bus pass, her school ID, her Medicare card. "You're only fourteen," he says. "You don't belong here, even looking for someone."

Lani continues to smile, even though she knows this is stupid. She is not a baby, she's been looking after herself for as long as she can remember. She also realizes that she is afraid.

Somebody comes through the door at the back, the one that leads to the toilets and an office or something. A cop pushing one of the guys in front of him. Bingo.

"Aha," Lani's cop says, "our man's still here after all." He begins piling Lani's things on top of her backpack.

"So I can go," she says, reaching for them. "I'm going to be late...." She wants to get out before they link her with the passport which she's sure is still in Bingo's pockets.

And Bingo's cop is calling out: "Kid's loaded: prescription blanks, seven IDs, a girl's passport."

"Not so quick," her cop says, putting out his hand to grab her wrist. "We're going to take you back to school."

They wouldn't let Rosie in to see Lani right away. There was some paperwork, the secretary said, the police had raided the school and three pool-halls. About ten kids were being questioned.

Not that they found much. While Rosie waited, she heard the principal telling some parent on the phone that even with warrants to search specific kids and their lockers, the cops had found nothing.

(Not surprising, Mitchell said. The kids would have dumped their stashes in the nearest trash can as soon as the raid started, he said. You might lose your stash, but you couldn't be charged for possession, he said. Rosie doesn't want to know how he knew that.)

The principal was pumped up about the whole business. It had been planned for weeks, he kept saying. It was an example of zero drug tolerance, of the way we Protect Our Kids. The fact the school was clean was Great Publicity.

But Rosie still didn't get it. She still didn't know what was happening. "Are you all right," she kept saying as soon as they let her in to see Lani. "Why didn't they send you to the hospital directly? Has a doctor seen you?"

Lani had her arms around this boy and both of them still

had their coats on even though the room was hot. She stood up when she saw her mother, so Rosie knew that her legs and all were working. And her face wasn't cut up, Rosie didn't see any bandages. She was so glad about that. She almost sang: oh my heavenly flower, how beautiful you are.

Her mother fills the door when they finally open it. Lani has heard her, yelling at the principal, demanding to know what the hell is going on.

In spite of herself, Lani finds herself holding out her arms. She's the taller one now, but her mother outweighs her by nearly 75 pounds. Her mother, who smells of frying and sweat and dandruff treatment shampoo, whose body feels soft, whose winter coat is ugly. Never is Lani going to let herself get that way. For the fifty millionth time she tells herself that her father can't really be blamed for leaving the way he did.

Still, her arms are around her mother now, and her mother's arms are around her. Somewhere in the background Alex is saying something. Poor Alex. Nobody has come to get him.

There is the matter of the passport, of course. The police said they'd have to keep it for evidence and at some point Lani knows she will have to explain it all to her mother. She knows her mother, her fat and ugly mother, will be furious, and already she dreads the day.

However, and it is a big however, for the moment she is merely glad to be safe and loved and warm. In a few minutes, when it becomes clear that Alex's parents are unreachable, she will persuade her mother to take him home too. Then she will walk between them, with her arms around both of them, in the gathering dark, under the light of the first star. And for a little while she will be as happy as she remembers being before her father left.

Peripheral Vision

If Shelley had mentioned anything about baseball caps and sticks with fluorescent balls hanging from them Marcie and John wouldn't have paid any attention to her. But when she came around to the campsite just as they were finishing setting things up, she was all nature lore and enthusiasm. Full of what Marcie's mother's generation called "pep," too. Nothing weird about her, at all.

"A nature walk," Marcie heard her tell John. "A night walk, to see the creatures of the darkness in their own surroundings, you know?" She was rather pretty in a plump way, wearing grey gabardine trousers and a short-sleeved lighter grey shirt. A uniform, yes, you could immediately see it was a uniform, with the insignia for the park and recreation service on her sleeve, and her name in big letters on the badge over her heart.

"We'll meet in half an hour in the parking-lot by the lake," she said. "Then we'll walk through the woods. It'll be a night-time adventure."

"What do you say?" John asked Marcie.

She dumped the onions into the frying-pan. The pasta was boiled, the powdered sauce mixed in, along with a can of tomato paste: they were ready to eat and would have no problem meeting the group. But at first she shrugged. The kids had always liked nature walks. This was their first trip without them, all three of them had summer jobs back in Montreal, and Marcie found it rather hard to forget about them, just as she could not get her mother out of her mind. This trip was an experiment in trying to live life without being encumbered by family ties. Time we broke out from all of that, John said when he suggested it. Time we started doing things we like to do.

Walking in the woods of an evening was a pleasant

prospect though. "Sure," she said. "Why not? I always liked those campfire programs." He grinned: he was game for nearly everything which involved learning something and being outdoors.

And at first what Shelley had for them seemed to be a standard ranger talk. She had a cardboard box on the picnic table in the parking-lot when they got there, and she was pulling out skunk and beaver pelts, while a tape recorder played the sound of night birds.

"The night around here belongs to these animals," she began, handing around the pelts for her audience to feel. She was funny and informative, getting the half-dozen pre-teens involved, fielding questions about adaptations for night-time: better vision, excellent hearing, astounding sense of smell.

When she was done she looked around at her audience: the kids who'd come in a yellow minibus driven by a woman who was holding her sweater tightly wrapped herself, two couples with small children, and ten or twelve other adults of assorted ages and sizes. "So," she said. "Are you ready for our walk in the woods?"

By now it was nearly dark No moon, no stars, everything hidden by the thick clouds. The lone streetlight in the parking-lot was bright enough, however, to see that the woman with the children wasn't keen on the idea of going off into the cool damp night. She began to herd the kids back to the minibus. A young couple who had come in a car also moved away. So did a man who was alone and a family with toddlers.

Shelley didn't seem to mind the desertions, though. "Now, who's got flashlights?" she asked brightly.

Among those of them who were left about half raised their hands.

"They all working right?" she asked, and their owners dutifully switched them on. "Terrific," she said, "now turn them off and put them away. We're going out un-technically supported. We're going on an adventure in the dark."

In retrospect Marcie realized that had Shelley not started talking about adventure, John would never have stuck around for what followed. He loved the out of doors, but he also called himself a rationalist.

And Shelley was suddenly talking about expanded senses. A few more people turned their backs on them and found their cars, but John and Marcie continued to walk with her across the parking-lot and then toward the bridge. As they proceeded into the night, she moved on to what clearly had been her subtext for the evening: peripheral vision.

Marcie thought she knew what Shelley meant, because her mother, who was in her eighties, had macular degeneration, which was one of the worries that Marcie was trying to escape. There was no hope for the old woman who had been living for several years in a thickening fog because the centres of her retinas were breaking down. She saw big things, she saw colours, and, paradoxically, she saw things better on the edges of her field of vision. She had, the ophthalmologist said at her last appointment, better peripheral vision than central vision.

Shelley began by explaining it: "You know, it's when you can see light better when you're looking out of the corner of your eye, rather than straight on. It has to do with the cones and rods in your eye, you can see it on the diagrams of the eye. And if it weren't such a cloudy night you could try it right now. All you'd have to do is look at the stars. You can see paler ones on the edges of your vision better than you can in the middle."

Yes, Marcie remembered something about that from another nature walk a long time ago, back in the days when the stars seemed infinitely far away and few manmade satellites circled the earth. Astronomy was filled with glamour then: a combination of beauty and an initiation into mysteries which had the enormous advantage of being solvable. Mankind stood on the edge of the universe. Our generation was going to leap forward into splendour.

But Shelley was saying: "Now, peripheral vision is a really interesting phenomenon." Her voice was so matter of fact, yet her words were leading them some place completely unexpected. "It is so interesting that these scientists down at Los Alamos who were working on preparing for space travel decided to investigate it. They were wondering about how people were going to get around on the dark side of the moon, I think. You couldn't look straight on because of the Sun coming at you or something like that. So the thing to do, they decided, was to try to develop peripheral vision. The idea was to concentrate very hard on something straight in front of you, and at the same time open yourself up to all the cues that were coming in from around the edges. So they rigged up this thing, sort of a baseball cap with a stick out in front, and from this stick a fluorescent ball was hanging. The idea was to go around in the dark, focusing on the ball which was right out in front of you, and then seeing how well you navigated."

Shelley laughed, and they all laughed too. "I mean can you imagine all these rocket scientists and nuclear physicists and what-have-you running around in the dark on the desert, chasing this fluorescent ball that hung just in front of them. It must have been something to see.

"But the amazing thing, the really amazing thing and why I'm telling you about it is that it worked." Her voice fell to nearly a whisper but her intensity whipped through them like a cold wind. "All these scientific dudes, even the ones who didn't think there was anything to it, really developed their peripheral vision. They could perceive things in the dark, they knew where they were and could navigate rough terrain when it was pitch black."

She stopped for breath here, and Marcie was sure that her eyes were shining, only Marcie couldn't see because by now it was really dark, there was no residual glow from the sun in the clouds, and the nearest streetlight was back in the parking-lot, a quarter-mile away.

"It works, it really does," Shelley said, as if that would convince them. "So what we're going to do tonight is an exercise in peripheral vision. It has the great advantage that it will allow us to get really close to the critters out there, to sort of slip into their world and watch what goes on in the dark."

Marcie looked over at John. She wasn't sure how he would react. Sometimes when he was launched into something he'd go to amazing lengths to see it through to the end. And Marcie was game. Marcie was fascinated.

The trail took off just to the left, at the edge of the bridge. It was a well-maintained path, Shelley said, but nevertheless it wasn't paved so they would have to pay very close attention to what their feet felt and what their ears heard in order to keep on it. And they should hold hands, all of them in a line, to keep together. She'd go ahead because she had more experience in the dark but it was up to all of them to pay attention. What they'd see and what they'd hear would be unlike anything they'd encounter in the city.

By then the group had been reduced again, as several others decided that the whole idea was either crazy or beyond them. That left eight of them: Shelley, John and Marcie, a portly middle-aged couple, two bearded young men and a young woman about their age, who might have been with them.

Marcie found herself between John and one of the young men. A car came down the road, switching off its high beams as it approached the bridge. For just a second Marcie was blinded as the lights swept over them. But then Shelley called out that they were ready, and they stepped toward the woods.

It had been dark out by the bridge but within five paces they were surrounded by black velvet. The sky, Marcie realized then, had been a slightly lighter black than the hills and the lake. The contours of the land had been visible, only she had not seen them. Here, however, there was no gradation between up and down. She could discern no outline of trees, no hint of topography.

Yet she could tell...what? That the path went this way, climbing slightly. The centre was smoother and more resilient than the edges. Her eyes seemed to be open wider than they ever had been, she could feel the skin around the bottom stretch. Her mind was filled with nothing but the effort to gather sensations.

"Shh," Shelley was saying. "Don't say a word. Just listen."

Marcie found that if she turned so she faced the direction they were going it was easier to get a sense of the trail, even though it meant twisting her arms to keep a hold of John's and the other man's hands. Marcie heard someone breathing heavily, she heard the sound of feet on pine needles, she heard the chitter of some animal their passing disturbed.

Then came a yelp from someone behind and the man in back of Marcie jerked at her hand. Some whispering swept up the line before he said softly: "Someone slipped, but it's okay."

Marcie whispered the message to John, who passed it on. They stood in the darkness for a moment. Then John passed the message back: "Not much farther," and they began to move again.

How much farther? Marcie couldn't tell. She found her footing more easily than she had at the beginning, but it was still a struggle before they climbed a small slope and came out into what must have been a clearing.

Here she could see a difference between earth and sky, or rather between sky and water. Down below was the lake, paler than the trees around them and the hill on the other side, but darker than the clouds above. Yet it was by hearing and not by sight that Marcie knew there was something moving there: a sound of water moving. Not splashes, not waves: just an intimation of a body passing through water.

Marcie wanted to ask John if he heard too, if he had some idea what it might be. Before she could decide if it was wise to make any noise at all, though, someone shifted his weight or stepped wrong, and a twig snapped with a noise that would be lost in the middle of the day. But in the silent darkness the sound reverberated across the lake.

There followed a loud report, almost like a gun.

"Hah," Shelley said in a stage whisper. "It's the beavers, slapping their tails. They don't like us here."

Another report rang across the lake and Marcie strained to see. She thought that perhaps she could make out the wake of a departing animal. But she wasn't sure. She stood there in the cool, damp night and felt the woods to her back and the water in front of her, the stars behind the clouds, the animals living their lives in the dark. Warning each other that they, creatures of the day, were there.

Beware, went the slap of the tail on water.

Beware. After a while they started back to the bridge. Marcie has no memory of how long it took. It seemed to her there were problems, that someone tripped, that she heard someone else cry out. There were a few moments too, when she wondered what would happen to them, strung out up the hillside above the lake, holding hands for all the world like Ingmar Bergman's doomed souls in "The Seventh Seal." How long might they wander around here in the darkness if they strayed off the trail? At what point would someone come looking for them? When would they decide they were lost, and stop to huddle in the cold, damp night to wait for morning? Could they climb in the darkness to a ridge above the water and then stumble off the edge? Would they...? But then suddenly they were out in the open again, and Shelley was telling them how wonderful they were.

"That is the darkest that it has ever been on one of our walks," she said. "You should be proud of yourselves, for seeing so well. You've made marvellous progress. You should keep at it."

Flattery, flattery. No-one said anything, but Marcie heard bodies stir as if shoulders were squaring and chins were being stuck out. "What you ought to do is keep trying," Shelley said. "This is amazing stuff. You'll find yourself opening yourself up to energy you didn't know was there. Yeah, and rig up a baseball cap and a ping-pong ball on a stick, like the guys at Los Alamos. Keep looking at it, and everything else around the edges will become clearer. You'll find your way, you'll learn so much."

Both John and Marcie were silent as they started back to their campsite, following the paved road and the circles of light their flashlights made before them. Finally John asked: "What was that? Can you believe what you heard?"

Suddenly Marcie found herself laughing uncontrollably as the strain of so much concentration dissolved. "We could have been lost there until morning," she said. "We were guinea pigs for a mad woman."

"She's a menace. How did she ever get cleared for park duty," John wondered.

And so for the rest of the summer Marcie kept one eye open when she read the newspaper, waiting to see a story about campers lost on the mountainside, or about a park ranger fired for leading dangerous nature walks.

There was nothing, however. Maybe Shelley was lucky.

Or maybe, just maybe, the reason nobody got hurt on her treks through the darkness was because she was on to something.

John scoffed at the idea the one time Marcie brought it up, but both he and Marcie agreed that what happened later on that night really happened. After they'd made their safe and flashlight-lit way back to their campsite but before she climbed into the tent, Marcie decided she had to go to the communal bathroom at the other end of the campground. Here under the trees it was nearly as dark as it had been on their walk, and on the way back she decided not to use her flashlight, to walk in darkness, un-technically supported, as Shelley would have put it.

Marcie opened her eyes as wide as she had beside the lake and she stepped carefully. And she found herself walking along in the dark, almost as quickly and assuredly as she would in the daylight. Not that she saw anything, really, but she just knew where to step. She even turned at the right place and made her way over the rough ground to their tent where John was already in his sleeping-bag.

Then in the morning she retraced her steps: beside the roadway was a ditch two feet deep. She had not seen it, she did not know it was there, but she had avoided it.

Strange. Very strange, and through the following winter Marcie wondered about it.

That was the winter when her mother's health declined further. Even though she lived some distance away, Marcie travelled three times to visit. Her sister, who lived closer, was there on a more regular basis. They were never easy visits, because not only was it difficult to see their mother grow smaller and frailer, but also because it was very hard to keep up a conversation with her, to entertain her, to pretend that things were not spiralling downward out of anyone's control.

Many times Marcie stood at the window and found herself telling her mother everything that had happened in the last month, from the price of the groceries she'd bought and the memos one of her co-workers insisted on sending through the various activities of the grandkids who were now scattering to find their own lives to lead.

Then, having exhausted the banalities, she moved on to describing all the travel she and John had taken in the last few years. Including the trip to the mountains and the encounter with Shelley.

How much of these monologues her mother took in Marcie did not know. Her eyes were always on Marcie, and at times her lips seemed to form words that might be echoing what Marcie was saying, but she asked no questions, and made no comments.

Except when Marcie scoffed at Shelley and her experiments. Then the old woman struggled with the words until she got them out: "Peripheral vision," she finally said: "that is something real."

The next time Marcie came to visit, her mother was beyond words: the family had been summoned because the nursing-home staff believed the end was near. It was late spring by then, and the birds were flocking to the feeders outside the window: nuthatches, sparrows, hummingbirds, robins. Companions in a darkening world.

Marcie and her sister babbled on to their mother about what they saw as the stood at the window: the flowers in the courtyard, the flitting birds. But by then it was clear that their reporting meant more to them than it did to her. She was slipping away quickly, as the days lengthened.

The night she died both Marcie and her sister stayed with her in her room. It was almost the solstice, the sky was light until nearly 10 PM, and they talked quietly in the gathering darkness. Gradually, however, their mother's slow and laboured breathing wove a spell around them, and they fell asleep in their chairs. Once before dawn, Marcie awoke and listened: the breathing continued, and then in a distance she heard a robin singing. Strange, she thought:

birds don't usually sing before sunrise.

Then as the sun was coming up her sister awoke to find that their mother was no longer there. Her eyes were open and she was looking straight above her, as if perhaps she could once again see. As if she would never have to rely on peripheral vision again.

Marcie pulled the old woman's eyelids down over her eyes, and she and her sister cried, two middle-aged women reduced to feeling like little girls. The way ahead was not clear. They held hands as Shelley might have asked them to do.

Frances on Breaking Free

We shall go in circles here, because that is the way life goes.

The first circle:

It is late afternoon on a hot day in the fall of 1912 as passengers board a westward-bound train in Montreal. The young woman—tall, brown-haired, blue-eyed—has wrestled her small suitcase and her small daughter down the aisle of the train to the washroom. The child is wide awake, having napped for an hour before they changed trains. The woman, however, is tired already, and she knows they have three days in front of them on this train.

What happens next is the sole story that exists in the family canon from the time when my grandparents broke with their families. According to it, my grandmother Frances MacNeill, after whom I'm named, opens her bag to take out the towel and soap which she has brought along to keep them clean on the journey from Boston to Saskatchewan. She coaxes the little girl, who is two, to use the toilet, then washes the child's face and hands. "Look out the window," she says, trying to settle the child on one of the benches at the end of the washroom. "See all the other trains."

My mother, who is the child, presses her hands against the window and beats on the glass. The train is not moving, but on the next track workmen are doing something to the brakes on a Pullman car. "Daddy?" she asks, pointing to the men.

My grandmother straightens up and sighs: that's where they are heading. Out west to join my grandfather, who had left six months before in an attempt to outrun tuberculosis by moving to a drier, colder climate. The tubercular rich at that time went to sanatoria in Arizona and New Mexico. The poor, who had to work as long as their bodies permitted, tried whatever substitute they could. Working on the Canadian Pacific out of Weyburn, was David Mac-Neill's stab at a cure.

"No, sweetheart," the young woman says. "Soon, though. And Daddy will be so glad to see us." She leans forward and kisses the child. "But you stay here now for just a second." And she goes into the cubicle, hoping to have a moment to herself.

For a second—or not much longer—my mother continues to look at the trains out the window. Then she climbs down and starts to explore: the sinks, which she cannot reach, the sliding lock on the door to the other toilet, the handle of the toilet itself. The lovely sound of the water rushing in from the cistern, the enchanting way things in the bowl disappear at the bottom. Much nicer than the privies at home.

'No," my grandmother says. "Grace, don't do that. We're in the station, and you're not supposed to flush the toilet." She struggles with her drawers, her petticoats.

Little Grace is giggling now. She's outside, looking for things that she can watch disappear down the toilet. The suitcase is open, on top lie the three pairs of white collars and cuffs her mother has brought in an attempt to look fresh over the next three days despite sitting up in the train. Before her mother has settled her skirts, the child has taken all three sets and flushed them down the toilet.

The story was told often when I was growing up. The nearly inevitable accompaniment was my father or his brother singing the words of the sign found in all train washrooms to the tune of "Humoresque:" "Passengers will please refrain from flushing toilets in the train while in the station I love you."

The reaction from the prudes who were my sister and cousins was shocked and delighted laughter. To mention toilets, love and mischievousness by persons now adult, all

122

in one story, happened practically never. We asked for it at every family gathering.

I was adult myself before I realized how startling the story was, not in its mild risqué-ness, but in the way it differed from the rest of the family canon. The difference is that it dates from the time of my grandparents' exodus and not after.

Many people flee. Many people that autumn were fleeing czars, landlords, famine, disease, sorrows of all sorts. Compared to them Frances and David MacNeill were lucky. They were young and handsome, of an ethnic group not ground down on this continent, of a religion that was dominant also. They were poor and unschooled, but smart. They had each other.

What they were fleeing is much more unclear.

After that trip west, there was never any contact between either of them and their families. No Christmas letters, no telegrams about deaths, no visits at mid-century when they began to have the time and the money to travel.

"A page turned," Frances would say and press her lips into the thin line we all recognized as anger. "We never looked backed," David would add and change the subject brusquely. There were never any tears shed in my presence, nor accusations made, but it was clear even to the children just what effort and pain went into that stance.

Why? I never got an answer from them or from my mother. It is only recently that I have put together bits like France's abhorrence of alcohol and David's fury at tales of beaten children. What I see is the outlines of a drunken father, frightened children, a wife in terror: things that Frances and David vowed not to repeat.

The second circle:

Summer more than 80 years later, also in Montreal. My daughter—green-eyed like Grace and brown-haired like that other Frances, but shorter than either of them—runs down the front stairs, backpack on her back, violin case slung over her shoulder. Mrs. Klein is on the sidewalk, making her slow, arthritic way up the street. Margaret smiles at her as she rushes past. Late for a gig.

"She's getting to be very pretty," Mrs. Klein says as she stops in front of the house. It is hot and she obviously is in no hurry to continue.

I nod, wondering as always if I should say thank you at a compliment to my children. After all, it is not me being praised: Margaret's sweet face has absolutely nothing of me in it. When she was tiny people always assumed I was her babysitter.

"So when are you going to marry her off?" Mrs. Klein says with a smile, and I'm not sure just how serious she is. Certainly all her granddaughters were married at eighteen or nineteen to young Hasidic Jewish men chosen by their parents. But she knows that we don't arrange marriages.

So I retreat into a laugh. "Oh," I say, "she's got to finish university first. She won't be ready to settle down for another three or four years." Or even longer, because at the moment she's saying she'll never get married. But how to explain that?

"She's at university then?" Mrs. Klein ask. "Studying music? She's going to teach?"

"Well, maybe but what she really wants to do is play in an orchestra."

"An orchestra? My goodness," she replies. "I'd like to hear her play sometime. I love music." And she continues down the street, her long-sleeved dress, her dark stockings, her wig looking even hotter in the sunlight reflected off the pavement. Someone from another century, another world.

A third circle:

Morning in the day-care centre. Margaret is just three and the youngest child. She is the only one who doesn't speak French and as I prepare to leave her she sits on a little

124

chair drawn up very close to the *monitrice*. Looking down, not smiling. With a red face and very close to tears.

Marc speaks English. I hear him talking with his father in the *vestiare* as he takes off his snowsuit. He's two years older than Margaret, already in kindergarten, a man of the world. And so I wonder if I should stop and ask his father if Marc might help look out for her, be an honorary older brother. But I don't because by the time I'm satisfied that Margaret will not cry again, the man is gone.

Three weeks pass before we arrive again at the same time as Marc. Margaret is doing better, she understands French even if she can't speak it. Marc and his father seem to be having a particularly bad morning, however. The man opens the heavy outside door for the boy, but does not come in, even though Marc stands just inside and does not move.

"Go on," his father says in English. "Get in there."

Marc looks at him and sticks his right thumb in his mouth. His left arm clutches a stuffed monkey to his chest. From the other side of the room I can see that his nose is running.

"Go on," his father repeats. But the boy doesn't move. For several long moments the pair stare at each other. Then, just as the father takes a step as if to enter, his right hand raised to shoulder height, the door behind him opens and another father with his daughter come in.

"Stupid idiot," Marc's father says under his breath just before he turns to leave on the blast of cold air that rushes in. I hear him, though, and so does Marc.

And that night when I come to pick up Margaret, Marc is in the *vestiare*, throwing the stuffed monkey across the room, running after it, bashing it on the ground, and yelling, "I'm sorry, I'm sorry. I didn't mean to do it. I didn't mean to hurt you."

His father hasn't arrived yet. I wonder if I should stick around, I wonder if what I suspect has happened really has.

But Margaret has a fit about putting on her boots, and we leave as soon as she is poured into her outdoor clothes.

I never learn if the *moniteurs* saw this, and if they did, if they talked to his parents or a social worker. Or the police. Later, much later, when Marc is a teenager and Margaret has decided she wants to be a violinist, I hear that he has developed epilepsy.

Fourth circle:

My grandparents' story, told differently, is romantic.

They met at choir practice. They both were young: she was eighteen when they married, he was twenty-one. For a long time I thought her family must have been very poor. Certainly his was: my mother says she knows he went to work when he was nine or ten because when she was in elementary school he did her schoolwork right along with her in order to catch up.

But the photographs tell a different story about my grandmother.

There are none that my mother has which date from the beginning of their life together. Oh, there is my mother's baby picture, but that is only of her, a serious little girl in a white dress sitting in a chair. Very much like the baby picture of my father, even though his was taken all the way across the continent in a small town rather than a city. Both photographs bear the imprint of an era, like the department store pictures my mother insisted on for her own grandchildren: the red Santa's elf hat and the package as props for Christmas pictures, the forest backdrop for summer ones.

The first snapshots we have date from after the First World War, after David's tuberculosis seemed to have gone into remission. They crossed back into the States then, into Montana, to homestead and so David could work on the Great Northern Railway. In all of the pictures but one my grandmother is wearing a hat. A hat with flair. She is tall and slim and her clothes fit well, even when she's wearing a cotton dress. Even when behind her is the one-room house they had on the prairie at Opheim or the sod house where my mother boarded when she started school.

I do not remember my grandmother as elegant at all. For as long as I remember she was a woman whose grey hair was tightly waved and cut short, who wore high-heeled, lace-up shoes, whose evening dress was blue *crêpe de chine*, who wore no makeup. Who showed, to my child's eyes, absolutely no fashion sense.

But now I look at the other figures in the snapshots and I see just how much more style than them she had. What she wore had quality whether she made it or bought it. How she stood showed confidence.

And she was a snob. My other grandmother (also Presbyterian, and born in the small town where they both ended their lives) might on the surface appear her social equal. But Jane McLaughlin was a farm girl, who kept chickens until shortly before she died and whose husband was a barber. It didn't matter that he and the president of the local college discussed philosophy with all comers Saturday mornings in his barbershop. They *always* were poor, whereas Frances and David made fortunes twice, in the nineteen-twenties and after World War II. That Frances knew how to behave both times argues that as a child she'd seen how it was done.

How? Not as a servant, I'm sure: there was never anything servile about her. And, on the other hand, there was a mention of at least one summer spent on Campobello with rich relations.

Ah, yes, rich relations who must have felt sorry for the poor girl. What a pity, what a pity. Families looking out for their own. Up to a point.

And here we circle back to the beginning.

I am imagining this, just as I imagined the details of the train incident. It is July 1908. It is very hot in Boston and

Frances Miller has run out to meet David MacNeill despite the thunder in the air. After the argument with her father, she twisted her hair up again, but it is coming down already. Her face is tracked with the tears she couldn't control in her anger. Her shirtwaist is spotted with blood from the cut on her mother's lip, her skirt is still wet from where she cleaned off her father's vomit.

David is waiting on the corner. He is enraged when he sees her, more furious when she tells the story. They will leave, they must leave. He will rescue her, just as he rescued himself. Their love will transport them: they will build a new life together. It is, told this way, the stuff of Harlequins and fairytales.

And in some ways, it is true: they do marry and by many measures live happily ever after. David does not drink until in old age his doctor recommends a highball in the evening for his heart. Frances raises the two girls and the boy without beatings, if not without harsh words and moralizing. The girls are lovely, and when they can afford it, buy the best. The boy, a late child, a child of prosperity, becomes a rich man.

Their marriages succeed somewhat better than the average. There are grandchildren, then great-grandchildren. David and Frances' living-room is full of photos, they send birthday cards, they attend school plays, they take as many grandkids as they can to Disneyland.

But David and Frances' children never meet their cousins. They do not know the names of their aunts and uncles until David, a widower and over 90, is coaxed one day into naming them. By then he is sure they are dead: he believes he is the survivor. He and Frances have won.

And now the last circle.

This spring the last of the half-dozen Hasidic neighbour girls my daughter's age will marry. Margaret and I have watched each of them in turn parade past with their new diamonds, seen their mothers consulting about apartments and clothes and kitchen equipment. We've watched them go off to their weddings in the late afternoon, wearing gorgeous white wedding dresses, and come back to visit the next day or a day later walking beside a black-coated, black-hatted boy. Laughing and talking often. Looking at the pavement sometimes. And once red-faced and close to tears, or so it seemed to me.

Margaret, however, will choose her own partner for good or ill as our people have done for the last 150 or 200 years. She is in no hurry: she has her music, she wants to travel. She is not trying to escape something, and the boys she grew up with are just that: still boys, not yet men.

Boys: I ran into Marc's father in the grocery store a while ago. He said Marc was out on the West Coast with his mother, finishing up high school. He said that he was adjusting pretty well to having to take medication and that the epilepsy was under control. He said that he was turning out to be one damn fine kid.

Margaret doesn't remember him. Just as well, my Mother-Hen heart says. One less cycle, one less circle that she might have been caught up in. How hard it is to break free.

3

The Various Colours of Hope

Cold Comfort

Carole's breath froze instantly when it touched the inside of the windshield. She tried to keep a space on the glass clear so she could look out but it was hard, scraping with her left hand while she steered with her right.

All day and all night Friday it had snowed: the first snow of the year, heavy wet snow that froze to form a crust when an Arctic front swept down Saturday. Now, near four o'clock on the night between Saturday and Sunday, she wished Volkswagens had better heaters. Her feet were frozen despite her winter boots. Her parka kept the top of her body relatively warm but the black *crêpe de chine* trousers she wore playing piano in the bar were cold.

The streetlights glistened off the crust on the snow in the park: no-one had walked on it, it looked like a sheet of diamonds. Which meant that there was no-one in the park. Good. She didn't see anyone on the sidewalk, either, not in this *temps de loup*, this wolf weather. Most of the time she succeeded in not being afraid when she drove home late, but she was always glad for confirmation that things were okay.

The light at Park and Mount Royal avenues was red and she stopped. The wind roared down from the top of the mountain, shaking the VW. A police car went by, going from west to east, with hood lights flashing but sirens silent. It slowed down at the intersection but didn't stop; didn't matter because the only other moving car was one way up the hill.

Ben said she was nuts to drive home by herself: take a taxi, you don't need a car really. Or get another job. He didn't seem to appreciate how perfect the set up was: she earned enough playing Thursday, Friday and Saturday to pay her way at the McGill music school as long as her

132

mother took care of Annie. But then maybe she shouldn't expect him to understand. She'd decided when she moved in next to him that she wanted to keep him out of her life. The last thing she needed now that she was finally on her own was another man.

The wind shook the car again, bringing with it a fine spray of snow picked up from the ground somewhere. Driving down to Ormstown to see her mother and Annie was going to be pretty bad. She ought to call before she set out to see what road conditions were. Blowing snow was often worse than the actual storm and country roads could be more dangerous than here, even late at night. There she could spin around on black ice and smash into a tree or an oncoming car and spray her brains all over the road and....

Up ahead it looked like something was happening, though. Cars were double parked on both sides of the street around the next intersection and the Esso station seemed transformed into a parking-lot. She bought gas there ordinarily; the kid who worked there most evenings was friendly and she liked that. But now the station lights were out, and the place looked desolate.

The light turned green for her, and somebody ran across the street. Somebody else followed and jumped into the back of a white limousine.

One of the men on the corner of the service station lot turned around just then, and for a second, she thought it was Eddie, her ex-husband: his parka looked like the one Eddie was wearing the last winter they were together. But of course, it wouldn't be Eddie. He was in Calgary, the last she'd heard, and he wouldn't still be wearing something that was at least five years old. Not if he could help it.

Nevertheless, she felt a psychic cold creep over her, chilling her worse than the wind or the wicked temperature.

But she only had three more blocks to go, then a right

turn onto a side street, a left turn into the lane and there she was: home. Tomorrow she'd sleep in. Tomorrow she'd spend some time on her own music before she went down to Ormstown. Tomorrow....

She slipped the car into first gear and stepped on the accelerator. It coughed but lurched forward. Quickly she looked at the gas gauge: there should be plenty. She'd filled the tank the day before.

She listened to the engine, trying to decide if she could hear anything strange. Ben had offered to take the car in a couple of weeks before, but she'd said no, on principle.

Near the middle of the block, she saw a crowd coming out of the sports bar, the one with the four satellite dishes on the roof. Most were men in dark parkas—brown, navy blue, olive green, winter colours. But there also were two or possibly three women, one of whom was wearing a white coat. A fur coat, Carole thought. Full length.

Her attention was grabbed by the sound of her car, however. It coughed again, and lurched, then continued much more slowly than she wanted.

There was movement among the crowd of men. Noise too, that rose above the sound of her car, of the wind. Someone ran after someone else.

The VW stopped. The engine coughed once again and then died. In the rear-view mirror Carole saw the crowd of men surge out into the street after the fleeing figure. She turned the key in the ignition. She listened as the starting motor strained to turn the engine over. Ice in the damn gas line, probably: it was that cold.

The woman in the white coat was standing on the curb now, with two other women next to her. A man was coming up behind her. He took her arm, he tried to lead her away. She resisted. The other women stepped back, as if afraid to intervene.

Carole turned the key again. And again. In the rear-view

mirror she saw the white limousine start up, jerk across the street into a lane, back up, surge forward and then roar north, around the VW. Two other cars followed immediately.

The woman in the white fur was struggling with the man. Her coat fell open, and underneath Carole could see she wore only underwear: a camisole, stockings with fancy garters, all white.

Carole shut her eyes and tried to concentrate. She was going to have to push the car over to the side of the road, she saw. She was going to have to continue on alone.

She put on the emergency flashers, slipped the car into neutral and opened the door to get out. There was a laneway just up ahead. Even if all the parking places on the street were taken she could probably leave the car there until later. In the morning it would be all right. In the morning when the wind dropped, it wouldn't be so cold and the gas would flow again. In the morning this stretch of Park Avenue was perfectly normal. There'd be women in black going to the Greek Orthodox Church just up the hill, there'd be kids headed for the Mount Royal park to go sledding, there'd be no sign of what went on the night before....

The wind made the door hard to open, but Carole did it. Then she had to push with all her weight against the car to get it moving. The pavement had been sanded and salted in the middle of the street, so at first she had no trouble keeping her footing. But as she neared the edge, she ran into black ice, then ice furrows as she approached the piles of snow left by the snow-removal equipment earlier in the day. Still, the VW was light, and she could handle it herself.

Then she heard the sound of the men behind her. She caught a glimpse of the one in the parka like Eddie's. She took another step and pushed as hard as she could. The car picked up speed. her feet slipped on the icy pavement. She felt herself sliding. She was going to fall.

The men were right behind her. She struggled to right herself. She was going to have to run for it as soon as she got her balance and could reach across to grab her keychain from the ignition. They were yelling things she couldn't understand, and she wasn't sure it was because of her fright or of the language they were speaking. She only knew she should not, must not stay around any longer than she had to.

Leave the car there, she told herself. Don't worry about it, don't worry about your music. You've got your keys, you've got your wallet, go.

Far off she could hear a siren over the sound of the wind. She wondered at that, remembering the police car gliding by with lights flashing only a few minutes ago. The wind pushed against her and her face, her ears, her eyes stung in the cold. Maybe they want to warn them, she thought, maybe they don't want them all to be here when they arrive. She had reached the edge of the sidewalk now. She clambered up the frozen slush left by the sidewalk tractors, she jumped down, she began to run again, faster now because the sidewalk was less icy than the street.

A car started behind her, then another. She heard shouting, she heard a woman scream.

Then someone reached out and grabbed her. Someone who had been standing near the corner, who had stepped out of the entrance to a building or the bus shelter or from behind a wall. He wrapped his arms around her. She smelled liquor on his breath and sweat rising from beneath his parka. He was strong and she tried to remember what she had read and heard about self defense. She tried to knee him in the groin, but he was so tall she had trouble reaching the right place. Besides her coat and his parka got in the way.

Then he said: "Carole, stop it. What the hell is going on here?"

Ben's voice. Suddenly she found herself clinging to him, shaking, crying, almost hysterical. It was a long moment before she could say anything and then it was stupid: "I left my music in the car."

"Let it be," he said thickly. He put his arm around her and hurried up Park Avenue to where they turned onto their street, walking quickly even though it was clear the police were arriving and the crowd was scrambling to get away from whatever had been going on.

He opened the door to the building with his key, and then led her by the hand up the stairs to the third floor where their doors stood side by side.

"You shouldn't go in alone," he said. "You've had a bad fright and you look like you're frozen. Come in and have something to drink with me."

Her teeth were chattering, her arms and her thighs ached from pushing the car and running on the slippery surface. She wouldn't be able to go to sleep for a while anyway. A little company might help, even if he had been drinking. He didn't say what he'd been doing out that late, and she didn't ask.

His apartment was a mirror image of hers, only her living-room had the piano along the centre wall, while his had his drawing-board and blueprints pinned up on all the walls. There was no place to sit down either: the table, straight-backed chairs and the small sofa were covered with reports and drawings. He led her past the mess into the kitchen, and switched on the light. The contrast was striking: the counters were clear, no dishes were waiting in the drainer, the tiny table was covered with a clean yellow-checked vinyl tablecloth.

He pulled out a chair for her. "Tea with brandy," he said. She felt her face trying to smile at him, but her teeth were still chattering and she found it hard to control her expression. She watched while he filled the teapot, got out cups, saucers, spoons, honey, a bottle of VSOP cognac. The cups matched the saucers, the honey was in a little pot. The floor shone with wax.

He didn't come and sit down at the table immediately, but leaned against the counter and looked at her sternly. "Jesus Christ, I don't know why you put yourself in situations like that. Why don't you take a taxi home late at night, you'd be a heck of a lot safer...."

Carole sat up straighter and clasped her hands in front of her, pressing them together, trying to control them.

"Now come on, don't stop listening to me," he said. "I know about the job, and how it's so perfect, how you can go to McGill and work on your music and all. But it isn't safe. You could have gotten raped or gang-banged or God knows what. Those were pretty ugly guys out there...."

She saw the dark parkas against the snow, the one who looked like Eddie. She heard the wind, felt the cold. Felt the panic. And the nerves that had been wound so tight in order to keep her together and running for the last little while, suddenly snapped. She leaned forward and sobbed, letting the hot tears fall on her cold hands.

For a moment he stood, watching her. Then he came over and picked her up so he could hold her and comfort her.

When she woke up it was mid-morning. Even before she opened her eyes she was aware of the light, of the warmth, of a smell that was familiar and yet strange. She moved her legs, stretching into the cold place at the edge of the bed the way she did most winter mornings when she wanted to appreciate just how nice it was in the middle. Only the edge wasn't cold, and wasn't the edge. She touched something. She touched Ben.

The memory came back in little flashes: Ben's arms, and

his warm whisky breath, his mouth, his bed. Then the long warm expanse of his body against hers and their smell under the tent of the covers. His hands, her pleasure.

She opened her eyes and saw the sun shining through the pull-down blind. She was due in Ormstown by 2 PM, but she had no idea what time it was. She sat up. Ben lay on his stomach with his face turned toward her. His eyelashes were very long, she noticed for the first time. He needed a shave badly, and his hair curled around the back of his ears. She was not sure if she should scream.

He opened his eyes and smiled at her. He reached out to touch her under the covers, his hand gliding over her thigh as if it had already memorized the way to her centre. She felt herself grow moist and expectant in spite of herself. It had been a long time since Eddie, but she could not afford to think of that.

She took his hand and removed it from her body. No, she did not want him to touch her. She was angry. She had gotten screwed after all. And by her protector, too.

"Hey," he said. "What's the matter?"

She hesitated before she spoke. "Nothing," she said, because it was too hard to explain what she was thinking. She'd always thought he wasn't a bad guy, and how could she say it was all his fault? She swung her legs over the side of the bed and reached for her clothes. "Gotta go," she said. She started pulling on her underpants.

"Don't just run off like that," he said. "Aren't you hungry? I'm starved and it's so bloody cold outside."

She stood up and looked at him. Then her eye caught her own reflection in the mirror over the dresser. A solidly built woman, a little shorter than average height, with breasts that had begun to sag. Curly brown hair that stood out in a halo around her head. Strong—or as strong as you could expect a woman to be.

"Come back to bed," he said. "Please," he added as an

afterthought.

The reflection told her that she had a good many years in front of her, but not so many that she could waste. She did not want to get side-tracked, she did not want to be violated. She did not want to believe that she was going to get screwed no matter what she tried to do.

She sighed and reached over to pick up her brassière and her blouse. "No," she said. She didn't say anything more while she fastened the bra, then slipped into her blouse. She could feel his eyes on her, watching. Then she picked up the trousers and stepped into them. They were wrinkled, she'd have to press them before she hung them up. Good thing she didn't have to work that night because she wouldn't have time that afternoon. And this week was going to be tough: the composition for piano and violin was due on Thursday....

She fastened the zipper and the buttons at the back of the trousers. She looked at herself in the mirror, at the clothes hiding her body. He was still watching her, she knew. For just a moment she was afraid what he might do, and how she would react. There had been moments in his arms which had been pleasing, after all.

She would give him another chance. "I really have to go," she said. "Gotta practice this morning so I can go see my kid this afternoon." She didn't think she'd mentioned Annie to Ben; she watched carefully to see how he reacted.

"Kid? You've got a kid?" he said. He lay back on the bed and settled the covers around himself. "Well, in that case..." he said.

The anger she had woken up with flared suddenly higher. The bastard, she thought. But then she smiled at him for the first time that morning, because now she knew all she needed to know about him. "Don't bother to get up," she said. "I'll let myself out." She picked up her parka; her boots, she thought, she'd left by the front door.

He made no move to follow her, but when she was half-way down the hall to the door she heard him call after her: "Don't I get any thanks for helping you out, anyway? Maybe I could help you get your car started later." Perhaps it was a trick of the echoes in the apartment, but he sounded almost old and querulous.

"No," she called back, as she closed the front door. In a second she had stepped across to her own apartment. She pulled out her keys and opened the door. At the end of her hall, the sun was shining through a window which was covered by frost patterns.

How beautiful, she thought. She dumped her parka on the floor and went straight to the piano. She would have to take her chances She could not let herself succumb to fear any more than she could forget Annie or give up music.

She had time to practice for an hour before she left for Ormstown. She took it as a good omen that the car started on the third try, and, indeed, the roads were clear all the way.

Apple Time in the Committee Room

Hélène saw Ms. Herzog the night after the election just as she was going to the organizers' party. The old woman was coming toward her, smiling and waving at her.

Shit, Hélène thought. She was in a hurry to get where she could rage at the stupidity of the campaign planners and the perfidy of the opposition without worrying about what kind of impression she made on the troops. The night before, even after the candidate had conceded defeat, she'd had to work. There had been the campaign debt to think about, there still were people who'd pledged money but who hadn't yet coughed up. She'd hustled around, being nice to people, buttonholing contributors who tend to disappear when candidates lose, reminding them how well the party's candidates had done out West.

But tonight was going to be a different story, and the last thing she wanted to do was get sucked into a conversation with an octogenarian. It had been a lovely day, one last echo of summer before the world closed down for winter. Now people sat on porches; kids roller-skated; couples walked arm-in-arm, all suggesting that there might be more to life than lost causes.

But Ms. Herzog was coming toward her, walking as quickly as her cane would allow. She'd seen Hélène, no question about it. There was no way to avoid her.

Ms. Herzog had been born Victoria Purdy in the rocky hill country between the Eastern Townships and the Gaspé peninsula. In French the region is now called *les Appalaches*, and it truly is the end of the Appalachians with all that implies in terms of poor farmland and rural poverty. Her father was the third son, so there was no land, let alone good land, left for him. When the First World War began he'd gone to the city with his wife and their new baby. A baby named Victoria, after an aunt who had died young and after the late great Queen, of course.

But the Victoria was gone long before Ms. Herzog became a radical, long before she'd met Michael Herzog, long before she became an election stalwart. "A Queen," she would say scornfully. "Named after a bloody la-di-dah queen. I knew from the beginning that I needed a completely different sort of name."

An election stalwart: Hélène, who wanted to believe that politics worked, was always glad to see stalwarts, and Ms. Herzog was one of the best. From the time they opened the election office she'd been there every day between 10 AM and 5 PM. Hélène let her talk: she had a lot of stories, and she liked to have an audience.

"Tell us how you got your name," Hélène said more than once when she had a crew in to put out a mailing or do some other grut work. Then she winked to show the kids who were there that it all was cool, that humouring the old lady wouldn't be all that bad. Anything to pass the time, so much of the election preparations were a bore.

"This was back before my education had really begun, you know," the old lady would say in English. Then she'd pause and take the measure of the group to make sure they understood: you never could be sure in Montreal. She herself spoke five languages: English and French of course, but also Yiddish (learned from Michael Herzog), Russian (from two years they'd spent in the Soviet Union) and Spanish (started during the Spanish Civil War and improved working with refugees two generations later). More often than not in this campaign, though, she saw that English was the language to use. "I knew nothing about the world," she'd say. "My father was always working and my mother never got over the shock of ending up in the city. I don't think I even saw my old dad look at a newspaper until the

143

Second World War, when three of my brothers were overseas. This was long before, though: I was born in 1913, and this happened before I started school, before the end of the Great War.

"No, no, not like that...." She'd break off her story to reach out to stop one of the kids from licking the envelopes they'd just stuffed. "No, no, that's disgusting and besides you'll cut your tongue. Hélène," she'd said, "I thought I showed you eons ago, use a sponge for the envelopes."

Hélène, who knew about sponges but who didn't think anybody was ready to go to the next step, would laugh. "Of course, of course, what was I thinking of," she'd say, although for anybody else she would have been less cheerful. "But go on," she'd say. "Tell us about it."

Ms. Herzog would smile. "Yes, my name, I was telling you about my name. I was five or so, remember, and in the afternoon my mother would send me to the store to buy a pint of milk or five cents worth of potatoes or something like that, just to get me out of the house. That would give her a few moments peace while the kids who were younger than me took a nap. I didn't mind because it was an escape for me too. I knew back then that I didn't want to get caught like Mama, with a new baby every other year. I decided that about the same time I decided I had to change my name.

"But mostly I liked going because of the pictures. Now, you've got to remember that this was before television, back when the movies were just beginning. We didn't have any magazines at home either, and the only book with pictures was a Bible with only one, of the Last Supper. So these pictures were unlike anything I'd ever seen. They were on a building, running along the top in the front, and in this funny triangular space on the roof that covered what we called a front gallery. The people in them were wearing robes, and they were doing things like driving chariots and

144

holding baskets, and playing musical instruments."

Hélène usually glanced around at this point to see if the others were listening. They always were. There was something about the old woman that carried you into her story, even if ordinarily you cared nothing at all about imitation Roman bas-reliefs or the world of a child 80 years ago.

But Ms. Herzog was continuing: "It took me a couple of months of afternoons, standing out in front, to figure all the stories out," she said. "By the time I had, it was fall. I must have looked pretty strange out there, standing first on one leg then another, trying to bring my knee up under my coat to keep it warm as I stared at the pictures, making up stories about what the people were doing and where they lived. The last day Mama actually hadn't wanted me to go out because she said that my stockings weren't thick enough and there was so much frost in the air that I'd catch my death of cold. But I didn't pay any attention, and when she sat down to nurse the baby after lunch I ran out the door.

"Now, up until then I'd never seen anybody come in or go out of the house, but that afternoon a man opened the front door and came down the stairs, looking all the time at me. He wasn't dressed like any of the men I knew. He had on a brown jacket and trousers made out of some material that was sort of nubbly, and his tie was more like a woman's scarf.

"I froze when I saw him, as much because I was fascinated by what he was wearing as because I was afraid. I didn't think there was anything wrong with looking at buildings, but I didn't know for sure."

Ms. Herzog would have finished filling the stack of envelopes in front of her by now, and her hands would be resting loosely on the table. She would smile and look off into the middle distance, as if she could still see the man in front of her. She would continue:

145

"'What are you staring at, child?' he said. His voice was a big one. I remember shivering at how deep and loud it was. But he wasn't a big man. In fact, when he stopped in front of me, I came up almost to his shoulder, the way I did on Mama. 'What are you staring at?' he asked again.

"Well, I had to say something, of course. And since close up he wasn't so threatening I decided I had to answer as loudly as I could, in order to even the odds between us. 'Your pictures,' I said. 'The ones up there.'

"I pointed and he turned to see. For just a second, I sensed he was weighing something. Then a small smile flitted across his face as he turned back toward me. 'What a big voice from such a little girl,' he said.

"'So?' I said. 'Does that mean I can't look at your pictures? If you want to keep them all for yourself, why did you put them on the outside where everybody can see them?'

"'My pictures, my pictures,' he repeated. 'Do you like them?'

"That was a silly question to me: the pictures were marvellous and I couldn't see how anybody would not like them. But, of course, I didn't realize just how strange the building was. It was a Roman temple tacked on to a country farmhouse which was now surrounded by the city, a real odd duck. It didn't belong any more than the man did, but I didn't know that then. The forces of darkness finally succeeded in getting it torn down when the Metro was built: by then he was long dead too."

The old woman looked over at Hélène, who was now counting the filled envelopes. "Oh, it's a hard life, Hélène," she said. "You can't put down your guard for a minute or the forces of darkness will rush in."

Hélène nodded, but didn't say anything about the forces that were out there. "So the man didn't chase you away?" she'd ask instead, even though she knew the answer.

146

The old lady went on: "No, indeed, he didn't. He stood out in front with me and answered my questions about the pictures, about who the people were in them, and what the stories were."

"And what were they?" the young man asked.

"Fertility myths, I guess I'd say now. It was a farmhouse, remember, and the man who built it wanted to pay tribute to all the gods and goddesses of agriculture. There was Ceres, the goddess of grain, walking through a field, and Bacchus, the wine god, and Persephone, that poor girl who got stuck married to the lord of the underworld. She was responsible for the Canadian winter, the man said and laughed, and it was only a long time later that I learned what he meant.

"But there was one figure in the middle, who stood under the point of the triangle which decorated the roof. To my eyes she was the most beautiful of all the women: she stood taller and faced the world. She looked younger than Ceres and much prettier than Persephone and behind her were trees full of fruit. She had an apple in her hand and she was handing it to a little boy. She was the one I wanted to know about and so I interrupted the man. "Who's she?' I remember asking as loudly as I could, and pointing.

"He stopped talking and looked carefully at the figure I was pointing to. 'Oh, he said, 'just one of the minor goddesses, the one in charge of fruit. My father thought it was appropriate to put her in the centre because he grew so many apples around here. But what you really ought to do is look at....'"

"Fruit?' I asked. I loved fruit—apples and pears, berries when they were in season. I never had enough. 'Does she have a name?' I asked again. I felt something tingling at the back of my head. This is important, I was sure.

"'Pomona,' he said.

"And that's what I knew my name should be: Pomona.

She's a god worth worshipping, one who brings fruits and vegetables. And so lovely: I could just imagine her handing out boxes of apples and crates of oranges. Food for those who need it. Good food, nourishing food. Delicious food...."

The old woman paused. It was at this point in the story that Hélène usually wanted to laugh. Pomona was an amazing name, and to think that a little girl had chosen it for herself and then insisted that everybody call her that was equally amazing.

"Pomona," one of the young people would break in. "Like the American college, you mean."

The old woman would look at him contemptuously. "Yes," she would say. "I've heard of it. But this was so much more, so much more."

At his point Hélène would try to steer Ms. Herzog away from making some remark that the younger generation wouldn't appreciate. "And that's what started you out on your campaign to provide good food for everyone?" she'd ask. Hélène knew that the old gal had been widowed before she'd had kids, and had worked for decades in union education programs. Then, when she was in her fifties she'd gone back to school to get a degree in nutrition. From then until she retired at 76 or 77 she gave workshops to community groups, tried to start collective kitchens, organized meals on wheels programs, set up co-operative food banks. And complained, complained, complained about cuts in family allowances and the lack of free lunches in schools and putting soft-drink vending-machines in schools and....

"Yes, yes, but for more than just food. For decent income and housing and education. All those things." She paused. "Fairness too."

"And that's why you're in here helping out with the campaign," someone, usually a girl, would ask.

"Of course," Hélène said, before Ms. Herzog could answer. "There isn't anybody else to campaign for, is there?

Nobody who's got a chance, anyway."

And that was that, usually. Except at the end of the campaign when there were signs which Hélène should have seen, had seen really, but hadn't wanted to acknowledge.

That was when Ms. Herzog took up the challenge: "Nobody else who's got a chance," she repeated. "Does that mean you think that there might be somebody who hasn't got a chance but who's better?" she asked.

Somebody better. Well, there was a former Catholic worker-priest whom Hélène had encountered often at rallies and workshops. He was running as an independent, and there was no way that he was going to make an impact even if he was a good guy. On balance, Hélène would have to say that from Ms. Herzog's point of view, from the stance of a True Believer, probably he was a better candidate than their guy. But he was only making a point. This election would shift the balance of power in Parliament. To support him would be an expensive gift to your principles.

So Hélène said, "No, no, our man's the best. He knows the area, he's got the right ideas, he's a serious guy."

A serious guy: well, he didn't smile much but that was because he was generally furious about how the campaign was going. He was a union vice president, recruited to run in an election by surveys that showed him having a good chance to win. He hadn't known that he was going to be up against a well-known city councillor and the former coach of Montreal's soccer team. He'd trusted the party brass when they said they were going to run a professional campaign that would be long on principle and short on bullshit. And he'd been told there'd be a fair bit of money from the federal organization.

But it just wasn't turning out that way. The other guys were running to the left, as usual, even though they always governed from the right. What was worse, the people liked what the other guys were saying, and the polls showed the others' numbers rising, while his figures were falling. Hélène knew that the party gurus had just decided to put everything they had into the 25 ridings that looked like they still had a chance. This wasn't one of them, she knew, and she knew the candidate knew. No wonder he wasn't smiling much.

"A serious guy," Ms. Herzog looked at Hélène carefully and spoke softly so that it would be hard for anyone else to hear. "I've seen serious guys," she said. "This one is more afraid than serious."

That was all. She continued to help out, she was there to make coffee in the morning and there in the afternoon to tell stories: besides the one about her name, she told "How Fred Rose Became the First Communist Elected to Parliament" and "The Day Maurice Duplessis Died" and "René Lévesque Wins for the PQ." She even did "Tommy Douglas Talks about the New Jerusalem." The kids liked that one especially once they learned he'd been Kiefer Sutherland's grandfather.

On election day Ms. Herzog supervised the logistics of getting all the poll workers fed. "Food's one thing I know very well. Let me take care of it," she said. She did, and it was one of the few things there weren't glitches with.

The rest, well, the rest was pathetic.

"Hélène, how are you doing, my dear?" Ms. Herzog was saying, as she put out her cane to stop Hélène. "You don't look all that well. You aren't coming down with something now that the pressure's off, are you?."

Hélène would have marched on by, trying to pretend she was too lost in thought to recognize the old woman. But that was impossible. Just as that little girl had demanded to know the stories behind the "pictures" and renamed herself, so the old lady refused to be ignored.

"Ms. Herzog," Hélène said, "I'm in a hurry...."

"Of course you are, dear. You must have so much to catch up on, now that the election is over. But let me walk along with you a little. It's such a lovely evening."

Lovely evening! Hélène nodded, she couldn't deny that. But she didn't want to talk about the weather. She wanted to rage at somebody about how the party organization had cut them loose, to listen to others complain about lack of resources and too much glibness, to demand to know why the party wasn't prepared—again—for the other guys to run a campaign that promised so much, and to wail about the voters who believed those promises and forgot the fact that the promises were rarely delivered.

She wanted to know why she should keep on carrying on. Why she or anyone else should think that what they'd do would make a difference.

So she didn't slow down, but, to her surprise, the old lady kept up. "Yes," Ms. Pomona Herzog said, as they passed a greengrocer who was closing up, bringing in boxes of fall fruit from where they'd been displayed on the sidewalk. "I like this time of year, it was like this when I got my name. Apple season."

Hélène made a noise that might have been assent and might have been derision, but the old lady seemed not to notice. "Apples are my favourite fruit," she continued. "That's why I made up that story."

It took Hélène four or five steps before she really heard what Ms. Herzog said. Then she stopped. "What story?" It was dark now, but people were still out, talking to neighbours, stretching lazily in the still-warm air, watching kids on bikes make one last circuit of the block before bedtime.

"The story about my name," Ms. Herzog said.

Hélène felt something slip inside her, something slide down to clang against the disappointments of the last days which filled her heart. Her mouth suddenly tasted bitter and her head pounded. She saw how much she liked the idea of an old woman who had known from her childhood which paths to take and what things to do, how comforting she found the idea that some people are born with a certainty of purpose and a natural ethical sense. And she'd been charmed by the story, with its details about the pictures on the walls and the man who'd taken the loud-mouthed little girl seriously. That was the stuff of legends. "Why are you telling me this now, of all times?" she asked when she could speak. Then, after a second when she began to get her breath: "What do you mean, you made it up?"

Ms. Herzog put out her old woman's hand, corded with veins, and touched Hélène's arm. "I made it up," she said evenly. "Not all of it, but the part about the house with the pictures, and about being just a little tyke when I decided to change my name."

Hélène let the hand stay on her arm but she did not look at the old woman, and she did not say anything.

Ms. Herzog went on: "Oh, it's true that I was born Victoria. I really did hate being named for a Queen, I never did like the idea of anybody being better than anybody else. And I did choose Pomona for my name. But I was in my twenties."

She looked steadily at Hélène. "That makes a difference, doesn't it?"

Hélène nodded. "I thought you knew from the beginning what had to be done...." she started to say.

"But I didn't, any more than anybody else knows anything from the beginning. And when I was in my twenties, well, when I was that age things happened that disappointed me too. I had had great hopes for some people, for some organizations. There's no point going into the details at this late date, they aren't important now. But," she paused for emphasis, "I felt I'd been deceived, and I was about to give up."

"But you didn't?"

"No."

The last of the families were picking up tricycles and small children, and heading up the stairs to their flats where lights already burned cheerfully. The store fronts were dark now, and the harvest moon had begun to show above the tops of the buildings.

"Why?" Hélène asked.

Ms. Pomona Herzog squared her shoulders and moved her cane so that her hands, resting on it, were exactly in front of her. "I don't know. It would be nice if I could say that I had a revelation of some higher truth, or that some Great Man or Great Woman advised me to do it, to re-invent my life. But it wasn't like that." She paused again. "Maybe it was just the apples. It was fall then too, when I saw how things were going, and I remember walking around one whole day and not having anything to eat until finally, I stopped and bought a half-dozen apples."

The comparison with Hélène striding down the street, her head full of anger, hung in the air between them, but neither of them mentioned it. Instead, Ms. Herzog went on: "I love apples," she said. "They're there every fall in all their delicious splendour. Maybe I decided I had to try to match their persistence. Maybe I just liked the way Pomona Purdy sounded. Outrageous, isn't it?"

She smiled, but she didn't wait for Hélène to reply. "So I changed my name," the old lady said. "And then I met Michael and I became Pomona Herzog, which sounded even more ridiculous. The rest of the story just sort of grew each time I told it." And then just before she started walking away, she said: "I'm sorry I disappointed you. But don't underestimate what courage you can get from shifting the facts slightly to keep your spirits up."

Shifting the facts slightly? More than slightly, Hélène thought as she watched the old woman make her way down the block slowly, and turn the corner. Then she went on too, slower than before, less determined. Even more disappointed.

Somebody brought a bushel of new apples to the organizers' party though: a gift from a family in the Townships who were sorry that things had gone so badly. Hélène found herself telling Ms. Herzog's story then, both the old and new versions. Oh shit, she thought as she heard her friends laugh, I can't give up now any more than she could.

Protection

Three steps lead to the bus door, now just opening, and it is as if Ariane floats down them. She leaps to the pavement and stands in the hot humid air, as liquid, as warm as a bath. But it is not a bath, and she is not cleansed.

Then the 80 bus snarls away, and she realizes she is gripping the ankh that Richard, her father, gave her long ago when she was little. Slowly she relaxes her hands. Her sweaty hands. As she does, she raises her eyes and sees her reflection in the windows of the pizza place.

For a second the reflection wavers and Ariane feels dizzy: the heat perhaps? Or apprehension? Whatever: she is tempted to smile at herself, because she is not dissatisfied with what she sees: the legs sticking out of her cut-off jeans or the grey-and-purple striped top which is short enough to show a half-inch of her belly when she turns or stretches. To smile would not be the right thing to do. Claude, for one, might see.

Claude said to be there at three o'clock. No, he first said to be there at seven o'clock but Evelyne had protested. That would mean that they wouldn't be back before dark, and Evelyne said that in no way was Ariane to be out after dark with Claude. No way.

Ariane laughed at that. "Oh Mom, he'd never let anything happen to me. He says I'm the nearest thing to a daughter he'll ever have."

Evelyne, who was roughing out the clematis design with the satin stitch setting on her sewing machine, didn't even bother to look up. "He is nothing to you," she said. The machine whirred. She worked the material around, watching the design spread on the cloth. Ariane watched too, fascinated as she had always been. It was at least a minute before she spoke again into the telephone receiver: "Claude,

155

my mother says I have to go earlier."

Claude was not pleased, the impatient sigh Ariane heard before he spoke clearly indicated that. But he agreed. And here he is, waiting on the opposite corner. Even though it is so hot, he has a Navy blue sweater knotted by the sleeves and hanging around his neck. Khaki pants, boat shoes without socks, white, short-sleeved shirt. He looks more country club than Ariane remembers.

The last time Ariane saw him was at the funeral. Nearly a year ago, a hot day in September, the leaves turning colour, Evelyne gasping as she climbed the hill to the top where Claude has chosen to put Richard to rest. Richard's ashes, Richard's remains, Richard's *cremains*, as the man at the funeral parlour said.

Cremains. Ariane almost laughed at that, but she hadn't. She'd held Claude's hand then because he looked so sad, and because she felt guilty that she hadn't come to the viewing the night before. Evelyne had said she didn't have to, Evelyne said it was a barbaric custom, and she didn't tell Ariane that Claude had called to ask where she was.

That was the question Claude greeted her with the morning of the funeral though: "Where were you?" He'd been crying, his eyes were ringed with red instead of black, and his hair was standing out from his head.

"Where were you?" he calls out once again. The light changes and Ariane starts across the street. After all, what is Claude to her anyway?

He looks at his watch and then frowns. Last fall he was taller than Ariane, but now he isn't. Their eyes are level, and Ariane can see that this displeases him. But what does he expect? Ariane's not yet fourteen and Richard was six foot two; she's likely to turn out tall.

"I said I'd be here at three o'clock," Ariane says as she steps up on the curb directly in front of him. She likes the fact that they're eye to eye. "It's not five minutes after that."

She sees that Claude is carrying a shopping-bag, and that a flowering rose bush sits in a pot by his feet. A rose bush!

Claude leans forward to kiss her, and the girl hesitates, trying to avoid this conventional greeting. This is the man who loved my father, she thinks nevertheless. *He* appreciated Richard, even if Evelyne didn't.

When Claude steps back, Ariane sees that his eyes are squeezed together tightly. He looks foolish, although Ariane supposes that he is afraid he might cry. Ariane did not cry. She does not want to cry now, she does not want to feel very much if she can help it. She pulls at the wisps of her mind, calling them back from their disorder.

"It'll be a few minutes before the bus up the hill comes," she says because it is clear that Claude can't say anything for the moment. "We could start to walk."

Silly question: Claude has never been energetic. It was amazing that he agreed to take the bicycle trip with Richard last fall: that was part of his guilt, of course. Now he opens his eyes and turns so he can look down Mount-Royal boulevard. The next bus is not in sight. "No, *non*, we'll take a taxi," he says.

That is all he says, except for giving the cabbie directions, until they go through the cemetery gates at the top of the grade. "This is where he would have wanted to be, don't you think? We did the right thing?"

Ariane nods, although she has no idea what Richard would have wanted. She touches the ankh she has around her neck. Maybe he would have liked a pyramid, but how would she ever know?

Claude does not notice Ariane's silence. He directs the taxi driver down the hill and then up again to the top of the second little summit. It is the new part of the cemetery, grass-covered, treeless. At the edge, with a view to the east and north, stands the structure in which there is room for several thousand urns. A big chest of drawers for ashes.

Richard's final resting place. Ariane expects she should feel something at the sight. But she doesn't; all she remarks as she stands waiting for Claude to pay the cabbie is that up here there is a little breeze.

The structure is faced in some kind of shiny stone, with space for engraving names. It stands about ten feet high, in a partial semi-circle and the dead, if they had eyes, would be able to see the sweep of the river in the distance and the tops of the trees, on the slopes of the mountain directly below. But the dead have no eyes and so they do not know about the sculpture at the centre of the parabola formed by the curve of the structure. At the centre, at the focus point, as in the parabola of a satellite receiver. How many channels do the dead receive?

When the taxi has pulled away, Claude stands for a moment looking out at the river. "You can see it from here," he says finally. "I was afraid you couldn't, I couldn't remember from the funeral."

Ariane nods. She hadn't thought about that, but she heard Claude rage about the river when the news came that Richard had died in the recovery-room after the operation. Claude and Richard came back from Toronto on vacation, for a cycling trip: Richard's idea of course, Richard liked to keep moving. But they'd fought, and Claude had left Richard lying beside his bicycle on the grass beneath a tree, overlooking the Saint Lawrence. He didn't hear until a day later that Richard's choler was due to the pressure on his brain from the slow leak in the blood vessels at the base of his skull.

That happened in the past. Ariane folds her hand over the ankh. Let's get this over. "What are you going to do with the rose bush?" she asks. And as she does she realizes that there is no place to plant it. This is not like the older part of the cemetery where people plant flowers and bushes and even trees on the graves. This is stone and bone and ashes. No roses will grow here. The only flowers are those engraved around the names on the structure.

Claude looks away from the river, and sees what she sees. "*Merde*,' is all he says. Once again he squeezes shut his eyes, and for just a second Ariane thinks she might have to do something to help him. But then Claude opens them, and looks back at the view. "*Merde*," he whispers again. "I'll just have to leave it, just have to do it the half-assed way I always do things." He rubs his hand over his face. "Half-assed, do you hear me? Half-assed."

Ariane knows enough to be tempted to laugh, but also to know that the last thing she should do is laugh. She nods. There are no trees up here on top of the summit and the sun reflects as violently off the stone of the structure as it would off buildings in the centre of the city. It is a good thing they didn't have to climb the hill; it is so hot she would melt. Now, the thing she must do is get herself away. "You can leave the pot there," she says. "There, by the edge where there are those other flowers. We would have needed a shovel to plant it in anyway."

So while Claude stares out at the river, Ariane picks up the pot and carries it over to the flowerbed where petunias are wilting in the heat. The rose wouldn't look bad in the middle, so she carefully steps between the flowers and places the pot among the plants. Then she looks back at Claude; what else is there to do while they are here?

But the man does not seem to notice. He is still staring at the river. "You know he never loved me," he says finally. "I loved him, but he never loved me. I don't think he could love me."

Love, love: Ariane has heard much talk of love in her nearly fourteen years and she does not find it interesting or becoming in old people.

"He loved you, though. He often talked about you and your brothers. And your mother too." This last said in a voice that could barely be heard above the noise of the city.

Ariane makes a small, derogatory sound. She reaches over to pick up the shopping-bag. What else, what else, what else.... Evelyne was right, she shouldn't have come.

Claude has turned though, and sees her with the bag. "Wait, there's some things I want you to have," he says, grabbing the bag and opening it.

He pulls out a package wrapped in another plastic bag. It is about the size of a magazine, but thicker and heavy. "This is for you," he says, handing it to her. The masking tape wrapped around it does not break easily. Ariane tears at it, and is just about ready to try cutting with her teeth when Claude produces a pocket-knife. "Careful," he says. "It's precious." He slits the tape and pulls back the paper.

Ariane did not know what to expect but when the object lies before her, cradled in the remnants of the plastic sack, she is shocked. A book in a slip jacket with a small black-and-white photograph of someone's naked back on the front. She turns it in her hands to read the title on the spine: the slip jacket is covered in some soft material, almost velvety to her touch.

The Wholeness of Being is the title. So? she thinks. What is this? A self-help book?

"That's Evelyne on the cover," Claude says. "You'd never know it now, would you? Yes, that's it: open it up."

The paper is smooth and glossy, almost cold to the touch despite the heat. There are poems or something like poems on each page, with a photograph. Hands, skin, a breast, with the nipple dark against the lighter skin.

"He always kept that, he said that...."

"It's not Evelyne," Ariane interrupts. She flips to the front of the book, looking for a name, a date, an indication of where this thing comes from. But the title page gives names she has never heard of as author and photographer. There is no apparent connection between the book and the people she knows. The copyright date is ten years before she was born, four years before her oldest brother was.

"Yes, yes, it is. You'll have to ask her about it, if she's never mentioned it. But that's not the point. You should have it, because it was Richard's. Like the other things." He thrusts another plastic-wrapped package at her.

Inside are: a medal from a hockey tournament in 1972, a small picture in a black plastic frame of her and her brothers taken when she was a baby, a white silk scarf with fringe, and Richard's passport.

When she has finished she looks up at Claude. Is this all there is? she wants to ask, but doesn't.

"There were other things, old clothes, more books, things like that," Claude says, as if he heard the girl's thoughts. "I'm keeping the books, except for this one. The clothes I gave away. I sent your brothers his watch, his shaving things and some sports equipment. No, there's just this, that I could find."

This and an insurance policy, which Evelyne invested in bonds or something. But maybe Claude doesn't know about that. Evelyne was on the phone a couple of times, talking money with somebody in Toronto. A lawyer. There was some kind of settlement, too. But all that had nothing to do with Claude.

So Ariane looks at him and wonders what she should say. Thanks, maybe? Would that be enough? She tightens her hand around the ankh. Richard gave that to her directly, when she'd been little, when he left Evelyne's for the last time, before he met Claude, before he moved to Toronto.

Claude looks back at her. "You'll take good care of them, won't you? They meant something to him."

She stands there, staring at him, wondering exactly what he expects her to do.

His voice is rising, and his face is growing red under his tan. Emotional bitch is what Evelyne calls him. Have a heart attack one day, himself, she says. Ariane looks around. She is embarrassed, she wants to leave. Claude might dress okay, but what a freaking freak.

"Take them," he screams. "Take them, you ungrateful little broad." He stares at Ariane eye to eye a moment longer, and the girl feels the strain in Claude's body, the way her own blood vessels are working to their limit. Under his pounding gaze Ariane sees there is nothing left for her to do but pick up the things, put them in the shopping-bag, and start back.

This she does, without saying anything, without acknowledging in any way Claude's agony. She realizes the man's voice roars on, berating her and mourning Richard but she shuts it out, as she learned to shut out voices long ago. A lesson from her mother's knee, from her parents' bedroom, from Richard's own emotional depths.

When she has finished gathering up the things, she stands and looks back at Claude directly. "Thank you," she says, giving him at least that much. "Thank you." And she turns to start back down the hill. She expects to hear Claude yelling at her to stop, or at least for the level of the tirade to increase. But once she has gone a few feet, Ariane hears nothing but the wind, and what sounds suspiciously like Claude sobbing.

Let him, let him, let him. The plastic bag jogs against Ariane's leg in rhythm with the words. The ankh bounces on her chest. She wishes she had somewhere to escape the sun and the heat and the memories.

To go home directly would take no more than half an hour, even if she walks. But the shadows have not even begun to lengthen: it will be several hours before dark, before Evelyne expects her. Therefore once she reaches the northern gates of the cemetery, Ariane stops and considers.

The gates are grey stone with turrets and vines. They sit at the lowest point in the cemetery, close by the stream that runs from a hidden spring on the eastern slope. Richard had brought Ariane and her brothers here the year they had the dog, and they let the puppy run on the grass which swept from the gate to the stream. Ariane would run after him, and one time fell in the water. That was when Ariane thought the gates looked like they belonged to a castle, and Richard invented a story about the castle of Mont Royal.

That was a long time ago. Ariane knows now that there never were any castles on Mont Royal. She also sees that an ordinary, modern wire fence elsewhere marks the rest of the cemetery from the outside. The gates are make-believe, as false as the flowers engraved in the stone back up where Richard's ashes lay hidden his drawer.

She walks through the gates and continues down the hill, past the Jewish cemetery, past the well-groomed houses that back up on the hill, then down again at the intersection. She chooses not to take the side with the sidewalk, but walks in the gutter on the high side, the mountain side, the unkempt side. There are stories about how girls should not go into these woods—about how *boys* should not. Richard had walked there with the dog, and she had walked along beside him, holding onto the leash too. Richard told stories about this wood. Fairies lived there, he said. She now knows that he was making a joke that she was not expected to understand. that he was referring to a part of his life that perhaps he did not understand.

Her hand sweats where it grips the handle of the plastic sack. In the wintertime you can see through the forest. The black trunks of the leafless trees stand nakedly against the snow. There is no menace in the transparency of branches. Now, however, the greenness would swallow Ariane within three steps of the road, were she to follow that path there, or that one there.

Not that she had any intention of doing that. And yet, and yet....

She hears the bicycles coming, the sound of bodies and metal whipping through the air. Not the sound of the pedals turning or wheels on pavement, because here, where the slope was moderately steep, they were coasting. Just the sound of air slipping over them, like that of birds' wings beating, or of the wind. Something makes her turn around.

Walk facing traffic, Richard said. That way you can see them and they can see you. He held her hand when they walked along here, he wouldn't let her pretend to hold the dog's leash. You never know, he said. You never know at all.

There is a squeal as the first cyclist tries to brake before he slams into her. The second cycle swings wide to avoid both of them. There is no car coming in either direction. She has time to see that, she has time to think: thank goodness.

When she wakes up she tastes the blood first: like iron, like rust. Her mouth is full of it and something is sitting on her chest, keeping her from breathing. But she does wake up. She struggles through the liquid. She fills her lungs.

She finds herself with her hand around the ankh. The smooth surface feels comforting. It is as if she were protected by Richard's presence even yet.

Frances Has the Last Word

My azalea is in bloom. Defying winter, it sits in front of a window which is laced with frost. The first blooms appeared at the end of November, and with luck the raspberry-coloured flowers will last until the middle of January or later.

It is, it seems to me, a parable about life in a cold climate, about life in general.

To get an azalea to bloom in the winter you must begin the summer before. First you must cut it back, hard, as soon as it has bloomed. Then you let it spend the summer outside, in some spot where it gets a nice amount of sun and an appropriate amount of rain. Let it grow greenly, as in the Garden of Eden.

The Garden of Eden? Yes, I meant to say that. And, even though I am a non-believer, I do not speak of Eden lightly.

People supposed Eden to be a real place well into the sixteenth century. They looked to Arabia to find it because the Bible says that Eden lay at the headwaters of a river which branched to form four great rivers, the Euphrates, the Hiddekel, the Physion and the Gihon. Then, when they found no burning torch there guarding Eden's gate, they looked to the rivers of Africa, to India and, ultimately, to the New World.

But of course Western explorers found no such place. What they did find was a wonder of plants and animals. The searchers brought back samples, from which were made botanical gardens, small imitation Edens which delight and instruct, and defy climate and weather. Rather like my own window-sill, but on a much larger scale.

The azalea in my window was a present from my husband when we moved into this house. It bloomed bravely that summer and early fall. But then as the winter commenced it fell into a long depression. The lovely petals faded into little crowns of brown tissue paper. Leaves on lower branches yellowed, then fell off. It looked sad and hot, sitting on the sill. Outside, the green disappeared into a swirl of orange and red, which was in turn eclipsed by grey as winter lowered itself down upon the land.

It was a difficult winter for me: three small children, two hospitalized at one point. Around the coffee machine by the nurses' station, the old wives of all ages tut-tutted about the weather: no snow for the whole of January, an unhealthy situation. No wonder our babies were sick. Very sick.

I stood at the window and looked out at the other wing of the hospital, at the smoke stack from the heating plant, at the other windows behind which other mothers and other children waited. The sky was grey, the ground was grey, the bricks of the buildings were a dirty red that bordered on grey too.

Even the snow had failed! No white blanketed the ugliness. We were back to the palate of the world before Creation, when grey predominated, before darkness was separated from light.

I can still see myself there: stopped, frozen in despair before a tree-less landscape. Far, very far from Eden, it seemed to me. But at that point I would have liked to believe in it, I was almost ready to call upon the serpent in the Garden. Had he appeared to offer my children bites of the fruit of the garden's second tree, I would have negotiated.

The second tree? you ask. Yes, there was one. The Tree of Knowledge gets all the press, but there was another, the Tree of Life which would conquer death. No-one has eaten from that. Indeed, it was because God feared that Adam would, that man was expelled from Eden. "And now, lest he put forth his hand," the King James Version says, "and take also of the tree of life, and eat, and live for ever; therefore the Lord God sent him forth from the garden of Eden, to till the ground from whence he was taken."

In other words, it was decreed that from then on we were all destined to make gardens and to live with death.

Every civilization has an explanation for the sorry state of man. This appears to be the one most current in North America and Europe, and I think it is no accident that, despite being developed in a much warmer land, it still survives in this cold place. The resonances are all around us.

That year we got through the winter all right, on our own with no help from the serpent. My children lived, live, will live, I hope, long enough to plant their own corner and tend what they have sown. But it was in the midst of that grey season that I must have read Thalasso Cruso's *Making Things Grow* because by the time summer came I had learned from her what I had to do to have flowers in winter, and, by extension, how to live.

The trick, you see, is to touch the plant with winter, to make it believe that spring has come. Let the plant stay outside all summer, as I said, until you've brought in everything else: the geraniums, the ficus, the spider-plants, the hibiscus. Let it stay out until the trees turn colour, and the tomatoes die back. Until the waning of the force that through the green fuse drives the flower. Until winter.

Do not be hasty. To flower, it needs the brush with death that is the cold.

Then you bring it inside, and you put it in a sunny place. The buds appear almost immediately. You have done a small miracle, you have created an echo of Eden out of season. The blooms the plant bears become a symbol of how we challenge the Tree of Life, how we try to cheat the deaths which await us. Sometimes the great darkness comes very close, and sometimes we can escape it, hardened but beautiful, like steel tempered in fire. Like an azalea blooming in winter.

And that is the nearest thing to the truth I've found.

167

MARY SODERSTROM is the author of *The Words on the Wall: Robert Nelson and the Rebellion of 1837*; *Finding the Enemy* and *Endangered Species*, both of which were finalists for the QWF Hugh MacLennan Fiction Prize; and *The Descent of Andrew McPherson*, which was shortlisted for the Books in Canada First Novel Award. She was born in Washington state and grew up in San Diego. Since 1968 she has lived in Montreal where her husband teaches at McGill.